ALONE BUT NOT
FORSAKEN

ALONE BUT NOT FORSAKEN

HE HAS NOT FORGOTTEN, BOOK 2

SONYA CONTRERAS

Bull Head Press

Scripture taken from the NEW AMERICAN STANDARD BIBLE®, Copyright ©1960, 1962, 1963, 1968, 1971, 1972, 1973, 1975, 1977, 1995 by the Lockman Foundation. Used by permission.

Alone But Not Forsaken is a work of fiction. Although retelling the Scriptures' events as closely as possible, the real people, events, establishments, and locales are used fictitiously. All other elements of the novel are drawn from the author's imagination.

Published by Bull Head Press

Squaw Valley, California

Paperback ISBN: 978-0-9907237-7-6

ebook ISBN: 978-0-9990009-2-2

Library of Congress Control Number: 2019916281

Cover Design by *Damonza.com*

Copy edited by Titania Porter

Typeface: Felix Titling, Bell MT, and Constantia

Created with Vellum

Printed in the United States of America

I brought you up out of Egypt and led you into the land
    which I have sworn to your fathers;
and I said, 'I will never break My covenant with you,
and as for you,
you shall make no covenant with the inhabitants of this
    land;
you shall tear down their altars.'
But you have not obeyed Me;
What is this you have done?
Therefore I also said, 'I will not drive them out
    before you,
But they will become as thorns in your sides
and their gods will be a snare to you.'

— JUDGES 2:1B-3

This book of the law shall not depart from your mouth,
    but you shall meditate on it day and night, so that
    you may be careful to do according to all that is
    written in it; for then you will make your way
    prosperous, and then you will have success. Have I
    not commanded you? Be strong and courageous! Do
    not tremble or be dismayed, **for the Lord your God
    is with you wherever you go.**

— JOSHUA 1:8-9

Then the sons of Israel did evil in the sight of the Lord
and they forsook the Lord . . .
and followed other gods . . .
And He sold them into the hands of their enemies . . .
That they were severely distressed.
Then the Lord raised up judges
who delivered them from the hands
of those who plundered them.
Yet they did not listen to their judges . . .
But it came about when the judge died,
that they would turn back
and act more corruptly than their fathers.

— JUDGES 2:11-19

But He has not forgotten.

Samson's Story found in Judges 13-16

Dear Reader,

The Book of Judges shows God's people in peril by their own making. They have forgotten God. And by forgetting they bring destruction on themselves, yet they don't recognize their own peril.

But God does, and He prepares one to deliver them: Samson.

Even as Samson delivers them, they resent and reject him, bent on doing their own thing.

Though Samson does not show a stellar example of obedience, God still uses him. What an example of God's grace! By blessing Samson in spite of his disobedience, God uses him to show those around him that God is in their midst.

How much are we like them? We forget God and do our own thing. By our own choices, we bring destruction on ourselves.

So like Samson, we are. God wants to show us the blessings, but we limit what He would do by our disobedience. Samson gives us encouragement, showing us that in spite of our constant stumbling and disobedience, God can and does still use us.

But Samson also shows us another side. What blessings would God shower on us if we would just yield to Him **completely** and obey Him **wholeheartedly**? What strength and power would God show to the world by our **obedience**?

The world would know of our God.

Sonya Contreras

CHAPTER 1

Now the sons of Israel again did evil in the sight of the Lord, so the Lord gave them into the hands of the Philistines forty years. One man from Zorah, Manoah, of the family of the Danites, had no children. His wife, Z'llpunith, was barren.

In a culture where wealth is measured by the size of one's family and flocks, children are expected and welcomed. They become the inheritance, whereby wealth continues and builds. Because she had no children, Z'llpunith often overheard the neighbor women gossiping about her submissiveness to her husband. Even visiting strangers rebuffed her because of her barrenness. All this caused Z'llpunith to spend much time in prayer.

She found it hard to remember what the Lord expected, but Z'llpunith knew there was more to life than what she had.

What had she done wrong to deserve the Philistines' oppression, strangers' scorn, and her neighbors' rejection? She considered these things as she worked by the stream cleaning Manoah's tunics. No other women worked by her side, because she chose to wash when no one else would be there to judge her for her inadequacies and to remind her she had no offspring to take care of Manoah when he was old.

As she mulled these questions, she scrubbed hard with the rock.

She caught herself; if she continued like this, she would soon make a hole in his tunic.

Z'llpunith sighed. She had wished for so long to have a child. Every month she would pray, but every month she must bare the pity and disgust from all the other women, condemning her for not giving Manoah a child.

At first they teased her, telling how she must submit to her husband's needs for a child to come. But as the months turned into years, the gossip and tongue-lashing could be felt even when they were not present. It whispered in her head. And pounded in her heart.

It was a sign the Lord had forsaken her.

Manoah fared no better. He too suffered abuse from his family. Manoah took the razzing with a hearty laugh, and then drank to another family member's birth.

Z'llpunith heard them press Manoah to take another wife who would give him a son.

She bit her lip to avoid crying out. She feared he might.

But even when she offered, Manoah reassured her, "You're my only one. You are worth ten sons to me."

But Z'llpunith saw how he watched the others' children. She read the longing in his eyes for a child of his own. And she watched the light in his eyes die as the years passed.

She wept for what she could not give him.

Wiping her face with the back of her hand, she rebuked herself, *"This won't get the clothes clean."*

Just as she began to scrub again, a man, in shining white garment, appeared beside her.

She had not heard nor seen him come. At first, she wondered, *"How can he keep his garment so white? What makes it shine?"* But then, she clutched the rock tighter and looked for others. Was she safe?

The man spoke, "You have no children."

She looked down. Here was someone else who condemned her. But his next words caused her to raise her head to listen more carefully.

"But you *shall* have a son." He said it with such authority and power.

She wondered at his words, and almost missed what he said next.

"Be careful not to drink wine or strong drink, nor eat any unclean thing. No razor shall touch his head. He shall be a Nazirite to God from the womb. He will deliver Israel from the Philistines."

Z'llpunith wanted to ask how could she deserve such a child, but the man had vanished.

She blinked and stared again.

She looked for a footprint in the moist sand where he had stood. There was none.

She splashed her face with water, spilling it down her front. She looked again. Nothing. She had not dreamed the man. Had she?

She leaned back on her feet and laughed. A chuckle at first, then giddily. She splashed water high in the air and watched the sun catch the droplets as it fell back to the earth.

A child. *Her* child.

Her curse would be taken away. She would not be condemned by others. She could join their feasts without feeling isolated, condemned, and despised. She hugged her arms around her, squeezing her eyes shut as tears of joy escaped them.

Leaving her wash, she ran to the fields. "Manoah! Manoah!"

He left his oxen and ran to her. "What 's wrong?"

Z'llpunith was breathless. "A son!"

Manoah grabbed her arms to steady her. "Whose son? Slow down. What happened?"

"Our son." She laughed, even though out of breath.

"What do you mean? Get your breath." He looked her over, "No one is hurt?"

Z'llpunith threw her arms around Manoah's neck. "We're to have a son."

He hugged her.

She could feel his heart beating as wildly as hers.

His sweat combined with the smell of dirt filled her nose.

She clung to him until she had caught her breath, then stepped back to see his face. "A man from the Lord spoke to me. He told of our son, who will save our people from the Philistines."

Manoah squinted, watching her face. "You are well?"

She laughed again and met his eyes. "I couldn't be better. My curse is taken away."

Manoah nodded, hesitantly. "So you say."

"You don't believe me?"

Manoah wiped his forehead with the back of his hand. "It is so sudden—"

Z'llpunith laughed, giddily this time. "After 15 years of marriage, it is sudden?"

Manoah stuttered, "Well, no, but . . . you are sure?"

"The man promised us a son."

"You weren't dreaming?"

"See my wet face and head? I splashed myself to make sure after the message."

Manoah brushed a strand of her wet hair from her face and stared into her eyes.

"The man's clothes were white and shining." But as she spoke, she stepped back out of his reach and looked down. What if she had only dreamed it?

Leading the oxen to their headstalls, Manoah walked Z'llpunith home. The plowed ground was uneven. Z'llpunith stumbled.

Manoah tightened his grip around her waist and kept her from falling.

Z'llpunith felt a warm glow in her heart. She would be blessed with a redeemer who would save their people from oppression.

Manoah was silent as they walked. He had never been a man of many words. Today more so. His eyebrows were furrowed together, a sign he was thinking deeply.

Z'llpunith knew better than to interrupt him, but she looked at him several times as they made their way home. He never stopped working like, this mid-morning. They must prepare the ground for the rainy season. It required long days.

The oxen hurried to the barn, always ready for dry grass.

Manoah fed and watered the oxen. He gave them a final tap on their hind quarters, before turning toward the house.

Z'llpunith suddenly realized she had nothing prepared for his meal. She gasped.

Manoah spoke for the first time. "What is it?"

"I've nothing for you to eat."

Manoah braced her with his arm. "I don't need to eat."

Z'llpunith looked at him. After working hard in the fields, Manoah was always hungry.

When they reached the doorway, Manoah cleaned his face and arms in the basin. He grabbed the towel hung on a peg on the outside wall.

Z'llpunith saw the dirty towel and gasped. "I didn't change the cloth. Let me run to the well and get my laundry. I left it, when the man came."

He shook his head. "My hands are dry now."

They entered the house.

The dark interior smelled of the morning's flatbread and smoke from the cook fire.

Manoah sat on the bench before their table and stretched out his legs.

Z'llpunith filled a cup from the vessel inside the doorway. She handed it to Manoah.

He drank deeply, smacking his lips when the vessel was empty and wiping his mouth with the back of his hand. He set it down, leaning against the table. "Sit with me, Z."

He squeezed her. "Tell me again, what the man said."

Z'llpunith repeated his words, how they would have a son who would save their people from the Philistines.

After she finished, he sighed. "I wish the man would come again and tell us how we should prepare this savior."

Z'llpunith sat up straighter. "I almost forgot. He said I must not drink wine or strong drink nor eat any unclean thing, for the boy shall be a Nazirite to God from the womb to the day of his death."

"A Nazirite." Manoah nodded, yet the furrow in his forehead did not lighten. "But there should be more that we must do to prepare him."

CHAPTER 2

Z 'llpunith gathered sage in the hills beyond their pastures. Though her disgrace was gone, still she held her secret. Her basket bumped her leg as she walked. She hardly noticed as she focused on the distant bush on the steep slope. Its silvery feather-like leaves reached toward the clouds from its stout little bush. She climbed faster than she normally did. Did she have more energy? Or maybe just more purpose. She smiled as she adjusted her hand protectively over her tunic front. Yes, more purpose. She paused to catch her breath.

The sun had risen over the mountain, its rays melting off the fog from the night. She was grateful for the dampness, even though the dew wet the bottom of her tunic. She reached the sage bush and broke off the top leaves, smelling them before laying in her basket. The smells reminded her of the evenings when Manoah and she would watch the darkness settle over the land after a hard day's work as they drank their tea.

Manoah so enjoyed his tea. He would cradle his tea in one hand and hold her hand in the other.

Those were peaceful endings to a hard day.

But that would soon change. She smiled. There would be a child who would add laughter and noise and joy.

Manoah had been praying for the Lord to send the man again to give him direction on how to train the child. Despite Z'llpunith's reassurances, he seemed nervous, like he wouldn't know what to do with a child! All the village children ran to him, like fruit flies to the ripest fig. He would catch them as they ran and toss them high in the air, to each mother's great nervousness. He loved them all. And they knew it. Why should he be nervous?

But as he questioned his confidence, so her own doubts flooded her mind. Doubts that had plagued her since their wedding. Doubts that intensified when she'd had no son. Would she be a good mother?

She heard a hawk.

It circled the hill. What would it be like to see from his eyes? What would it be like to soar on wings over all the earth, without a care?

She stumbled. She had wandered farther from the village than she should have.

The place was peaceful.

But it wasn't safe to stray too far. If the Philistines attacked, they would like nothing better than to catch someone away from the village.

She sighed and looked back up at the eagle, admiring its freedom once more before turning back toward home. When she looked down, a man stood beside her.

She jumped. Why hadn't she heard him?

He was the same man who had spoken before to her.

She breathed deeply and kneeled before him. "Please, man of God, my husband has asked me so many questions since you came last. Allow me to get my husband, so he may speak with you."

The man smiled and nodded. "That's why I've come."

She took a few steps toward the field where Manoah sowed the next crop. She turned back, "You will wait?"

He nodded. "I will wait."

"Your news has brought us great joy."

Dropping her basket, she lifted her tunic and ran.

M anoah's stride lengthened as he hurried toward the man of God who had appeared before his wife again. His thoughts ran in circles. Which question should he ask first? Would he remember all that he wanted to know? A noise behind him made him stop and look back.

Z'llpunith had stumbled and tripped. She was breathing heavily and couldn't speak.

He reached down and helped her up. "Sorry, Z. I forgot you were with me."

She only breathed deeply in response.

He laughed. "I'll slow down."

She could only nod.

"I hope the man will still be there when we get there."

She found her voice, breathing between words. "He will wait."

When they were still a distance from the spot, Manoah saw the man sitting on a boulder. His cloak was shining white, competing with the sun's brightness.

Manoah slowed his pace. Was he worthy to speak to this man? He heard Z'llpunith breathing behind him. He took her hand and squeezed it, slowing his pace to walk beside her. "Sorry, Z, I forgot."

Reaching the man, Manoah asked, "You're the man who spoke to my wife?"

"I am."

Manoah's questions had whirled in his mind for many days since Z'llpunith had shared the news. Now they poured out at once. "When your words come to pass, how will the boy live and what will he do?"

"Let the woman pay attention." The man gestured to Z'llpunith. "She shouldn't eat anything from the vine nor drink wine or strong drink nor eat any unclean thing. Let her observe all that I command."

Manoah nodded. Before the news had seemed a dream. Now—it felt like it could be true.

Manoah's questions had taken wings and flown from his mind. Would he have another chance to ask? "Please, let us prepare a young goat for you."

The man shook his head.

Manoah's face fell. Why couldn't he even remember his questions?

But the man continued. "If you do, I won't eat it. Instead, prepare it as a burnt offering to the Lord."

Manoah nodded and turned to Z'llpunith.

She already knew his request. "I'll get the grain."

He nodded. "I'll return with the kid." He hesitantly looked at his guest. Would he still be here?

The man smiled. "I'll wait."

Manoah nodded, this time with assurance. He left to fetch the goat.

As he went, he mulled over the news. How could being a Nazirite prepare anyone to save them from the Philistines? Shouldn't the boy be trained as a soldier? Or at least have a job that would build strength, like forging metal? How could being a Nazirite help?

Manoah selected the young goat with care, making sure it was without blemish, the best he had. He carried it over his shoulders, as he would if it had wandered from the herd.

He strode back to the meeting place. It was quite a distance from the village and their fields. He must remind Z not to wander so far away. What would he do if something happened to her?

When he approached the area, he looked for the man. Not seeing him, Manoah quickened his pace. He was breathing heavily by the time he met Z'llpunith. "He said he would wait."

Z'llpunith breathed deeply as if she too had run. "He waits behind the boulder in the shade. The sun is hot."

Manoah moved so he could see the visitor. He sighed in relief. Who was this man who could give them a son when he could not? "What is your name, so when these things happen, we may honor you?"

"Why do you ask my name, seeing it is Wonderful?"

Manoah pondered the man's unusual answer as he lowered the goat from his shoulders and prepared the offering. He wiped his hand on his cloak after slitting the goat's throat. The choice cuts of meat and the grain he laid on a table of stones before the man and stepped back.

He looked into the man's face. "You have brought hope—not only to my people, but to my wife and me. Although you do not tell your name, I will honor you for the gift you have given. I feel unworthy for the mission you've given me. But I am honored to be chosen."

The man nodded. "It is in following the Lord's Law you will find your strength."

Manoah nodded, unsure how God's Words could give strength against the Philistines, but he believed. This man held power by his words. They would come to pass.

Suddenly, flames shot into the sky, rising into heaven as if to God's very throne. Manoah fell back and watched as the smoke thinned and disappeared. Where had the fire gotten its power?

The man was gone!

Manoah fell with his face in the dirt. "Surely we will die, for we have seen God."

Z'llpunith lifted her face from the ground and reached for Manoah's hand. "If the Lord wanted to kill us, He wouldn't have accepted our burnt and grain offerings."

He looked at the rocks where the grain and meat offering had been placed.

Nothing was left; even the rocks had been burned.

She continued. "Nor would He have shown us these great things and promised us a son." Her face glowed at the final words.

Manoah smiled. "We will honor God, Who is Wonderful."

CHAPTER 3

Z'llpunith finished grinding the grain for the day's flatbread. How much would she be able to eat, anyway? Her insides were knotted and unsettled. Being engrossed in her thoughts, she had not heard anything until she looked up. "Renata! You startled me!" Z'llpunith pushed herself up from the ground with effort and tried to mask her nauseousness with a smile.

Renata laughed as she embraced Z'llpunith. "I've come with news." She was breathless. Her face glowed with a shine not given by the walk. "I'm with child!"

Z'llpunith swallowed. Usually she received this news with resentment, forcing a smile and an enthusiastic embrace. But this time, she genuinely smiled. She could share with her sister's joy as the baby grew inside her as well. But she would hold her secret for just a little longer to allow her sister the attention, though this was her fifth child. "You are truly blessed." She held her at arms-length. "How are you feeling?"

Renata's smile grew. "This one hardly bothers me. I can eat anything I want. Although I've been craving matza smeared with honey."

That's what would settle her insides! "That's it!"

Renata looked at her sharply.

Z'llpunith tried to cover her outburst. "I've been craving something sweet lately. That's what I want."

Renata's eyes narrowed. "If I didn't know better—" She paused and studied Z'llpunith. "I'd think you were also with child."

Z'llpunith felt her cheeks flush. She looked away and shrugged. "Anyone can want sweet crackers without being with child."

Renata nodded, but stepped back, still watching Z'llpunith. "But wanting sweets doesn't give you a glow. Z, are you?"

She wouldn't lie, but she did not want her news scattered to everyone yet. Z'llpunith hesitated too long.

"You are!" Renata pulled her into another hug. "Z, it's about time."

Z'llpunith felt her face grow hot. "Oh, Renata, what Manoah and I do is not for everyone to talk about."

"Oh, but you're wrong. It has been. I'm glad you figured it out."

Z'llpunith shook her head. Must all the women discuss her marriage as if they had nothing better to do?

"Are you sick? When will it come? How is Manoah with the news?"

Z'llpunith laughed. "Sit and I will tell you." Her heart warmed to the subject. Maybe having Renata know would help. Just thinking of eating matza had made her insides settle.

Z'llpunith rested after bringing the water needed for the day. It sat inside the doorway to stay cool out of the sun for her needs later. The day had already grown hot.

She felt a listlessness she could not describe. She rubbed her growing womb. Had it already been six moon cycles since her disgrace was taken away? She must weave another tunic to fit over her growing belly. Even her cloak, though not needed now in the hot days of summer, would not fit around her.

But that was not why she felt uneasy. She had so many more fears than before. Was the baby developing right in her womb? Would she be a good mother? Would she even know what to do? When she had held babies, she felt awkward. Would she feel like that with her own child? She didn't share what she had thought would help with other children. What experience did she have? But what would she do with her own? Did knowing come with just having? Her thoughts were interrupted by a kick, followed by another. She rested her hand where his foot extended. Who would this man child be?

She glanced at the rug which hid the door where their wines aged in a cellar. Z'llpunith loved the delicate flavor of wine. She didn't favor the harsher, stronger power of other drinks that were fermented and aged to bring a richer flavor, but wine had a soft flavor she enjoyed. She licked her lips, tasting their saltiness.

When the angel of the Lord had told her she could not drink wine, she thought it would be easy. Hadn't she promised God she would do anything if He would give her a child?

Now, she wished for a sip to calm her. She could become so nervous over what to do tomorrow. She sighed. Just do what she must today. She tore her gaze away from the hidden door, instead taking a gulp of the water from the dipper. Its coldness helped her focus. She wiped her mouth with her hand.

And what must she do today? She saw the matza dough resting on her work table and sighed. Initially matzo had sounded so good. And it did help. Manoah had even started taking it when he checked his herds.

But how many crackers can a person eat before he becomes a cracker?

She looked out the doorway again at the bright sunshine and gentle breeze stirring the fig trees that shaded her doorway. She noticed Renata running. Her face was red, blotchy from crying. Z'llpunith ran to the doorway. "Renata, what is it?"

"My child is gone!"

Z'llpunith felt as if her own child had left her. What could she say that would ease the pain? She hugged her.

Before, she'd recite Job's words, "The Lord gives and the Lord takes away. Blessed be the name of the Lord." But could she say those words if her own son were taken away?

She held Renata tightly. Her own growing baby hindering a tight hug.

Her sister pulled away, looking down.

Z'llpunith touched her womb. The pain of her sister's loss more evident by her own gain.

What would life be like if it was she who had lost her son?

She would rather die with her son than live.

The desire for a sip of wine to calm her own fears was strong. She breathed deeply and wiped a lose strand of Renata's hair from her face. Who could understand God's ways?

Manoah's prayer came to mind. "We will honor the God Who is Wonderful."

Although she still felt her sister's pain, her fears slipped away, the desire for wine disappeared and a peace surrounded her that the God Who is Wonderful would protect her child until their people were free.

The time came when Z'llpunith delivered a son. Manoah called him Samson. Z'llpunith swallowed the lump in her throat as Manoah gazed on Samson with such pride and devotion as he held him. When Samson grabbed his big finger with his little hand, she thought her heart would burst. She could not imagine a happier household.

When Samson required her attention, she gave it without hesitation. She seemed to know what he needed, even before he cried to tell her.

The older, not-so-busy women who had grown children gossiped from a distance, but their words sifted back to Z'llpunith. "She dotes on him." "He's spoiled." "She carries him around all the time. He'll never learn to walk."

She ignored their prattle and gloried in each phase of Samson's life.

His first smile.

His first coo.

His first step.

Manoah was just as excited. Oh, what a wonderful father he was!

Manoah told his wife, "I don't want you to cut my hair anymore. If my son must be separate unto God, I, as his abba, must be the example." His hair grew and became a symbol to those in the village of his dedication. But even more than just an outside change, he followed the man's words and learned the Law, as he told Z'llpunith, "God's Law gives me the strength to help Samson." Z'llpunith watched the Law change Manoah. He grew a quiet dependence upon God that gave security and inner strength.

Z'llpunith leaned on that strength for what she knew would come.

.

CHAPTER 4

TWELVE YEARS LATER

Samson wiped his hand down his tunic to remove the dirt. He noticed that the dirt smudged his tunic, but he didn't care. He just hoped his mother wouldn't see it and make him clean up before they left for the gathering. Family gatherings were so bothersome!

"Samson, let me fix your hair."

"*Ima*, it's fine."

Z'llpunith held the brush waiting.

He sighed and moved so she could fix his hair.

"Ouch."

"If you would brush it every day, it wouldn't have branches, leaves, and—what's this?" She held up something. "A nest?"

Samson turned, even as she clung to his hair and pulled the nest from her hand, tucking it into his pocket. "Nothing, *Ima*."

She stopped brushing. "How did it get in your hair?"

"I put it there."

"Why?"

She would not stop until she knew. He mumbled, "It's kindling when I burn things."

"You could burn the entire village!"

Why did his *ima* overreact? "I don't go to the village."

She brushed his hair again. "These knots wouldn't be so bad if you didn't put nests in your hair."

"It's easier to carry, and then I won't forget it."

"So, what do you burn?"

He should have known the conversation wasn't finished. "I cook meat."

"Where do you get meat?"

Samson sighed. This was going to be one of those long talks. Especially since she had only begun to get his knots out. "*Ima*, why can't I cut my hair? It would make it easier for you."

It was her turn to sigh. "As we've told you before, the angel of the Lord instructed us to follow the Nazarite vow. No wine. No touching dead things. No cutting hair."

"It seems so much work." He turned his eyes up to her. "I mean for you."

His *ima* smiled. "It's not work when I do something for those I love."

Samson made sure she saw his smile. Perhaps he had avoided another long talk.

His *ima* sighed. "Samson—"

Maybe not. He waited.

"Today at the festivities—"

"*Ima*, that reminds me, my head always hurts."

His *ima* lifted the braids off his neck.

It instantly brought a coolness to his neck and the strain seemed lighter.

She felt his forehead with the back of her hand. "If you stop using your hair to carry things, you wouldn't have so much weight. Although your hair does weigh a lot . . . Samson, today at the festivities—"

He had not succeeded. He sighed inwardly.

"Could you *try* to play with your cousins and the other boys?"

Samson made his eyes big and his face expressionless. "Of course."

She let go of his last braid and turned toward the door. "Please carry the basket." She seemed to reconsider, then said, "Carefully."

Samson grabbed the basket by the door. It held his baby brother, Tad, who had been a surprise to the whole village. He carried it with care until he reached the families already gathering, and saw his cousins at the edge of the forest. Maybe they would play something interesting today. He ran.

The basket swung from his arm in rhythm with his feet.

As he reached the group, he heard his *ima* call, "Samson!"

She was standing by the other women. She gestured for the basket.

He looked at his arm.

The baby swung wildly and cooed.

As he walked toward his *ima,* he overheard the other women.

"What if he'd tripped and the baby fell out?"

"You need to control that boy, Z'llpunith."

His *ima's* forehead wrinkled, a sure sign she was not happy.

He handed her the basket. "Sorry, Ima, I forgot."

She pushed his braid to his back and whispered, "Thank you, Son."

As he returned to the boys, he remembered his *ima*'s other request. He would try hard to do what she asked.

The boys had already formed teams.

Samson yelled, "What team am I on?"

Ahiezer, the leader of the first team, looked him over. "We don't need any small boys on our team."

Samson started walking toward the second team.

But when he was almost there, the second team's leader said, "We don't want you, either. Go look for the angel that promised you a mission."

His story had been shared many times since the angel had come. It seemed more a curse than a blessing. "What game are you playing?"

Ahiezer shrugged. "Not that it's any concern to you. They're the Philistines, we're the Israelites."

Samson nodded. He watched each team run for the woods. This game he could play. He would be his own team. He shook out a loop of string from his tunic pocket and hunted down each boy, one-by-one. He tied each captive and took them to a cave he was sure only he knew.

When the bell rang for dinner, he ran to eat.

Samson filled his flatbread with grilled meat and vegetables and ate hungrily. This was the best part of gatherings.

The women looked around for their sons, calling for them to come to eat.

Samson had finished several flatbreads loaded with food and was wiping his hands down his tunic when his *abba* approached him. "Samson." His voice was low.

"Yes?"

"Where are the other boys?"

He looked around. All the fathers and mothers were watching him.

His *ima* looked like she was about to cry.

He was the only boy there. Guess he had caught them all. "We were playing."

His father's voice held an edge, "Samson, where are the other boys?"

Samson shrugged. "Tied in a cave."

"All of them?"

Samson smiled sheepishly. "I guess that means I won."

His father tried to hide a smile. "Yes, now go release your captives."

"Yes, *Abba.*"

Samson paused at the cave's entrance to allow his eyes to adjust before untying each boy. Why should he let them go?

He sighed as his *ima*'s tears came to mind.

After each boy was freed, they left quickly, without a word. Samson waited until last to untie the leaders of the teams.

Ahiezer glared at Samson as he untied him. He stood and rubbed his wrists where the cords had been tied. "It's beyond me how a tiny *boy* like you could overpower all of us." He began to walk away.

Samson ignored him. He would not answer an insult. He shook the cords he had used to tie his prisoners.

While his head was turned, Ahiezer yanked him by his braids and threw him to the ground. He pounded his face and stomach.

An uncontrolled rage surged through Samson. He twisted and turned, squeezing out from under Ahiezer, then punched with both hands. "No one, and I mean, no one, touches my hair. Got it?"

"Samson!" His father's voice penetrated through his rage.

Samson glanced up from his straddled position over Ahiezer.

His father stood with the other fathers and their boys at the cave's entrance.

Samson dropped his fist. His shoulders sagged. He stood.

The leader scrambled from the ground and hid within the group.

Manoah firmly held Samson's shoulder and waited. When the others were gone, Manoah spoke, "Samson." His tone held a plea, a question and exasperation, all in one.

Samson looked into his father's face and shrugged. "I didn't start it. He touched my hair."

They left the feast. The walk home was quiet; everyone felt the tension. Manoah's normal pace could not compare to the speed at which Z'llpunith ran home. He hurried to keep beside her.

When they reached home, Manoah placed the basket on the table. His gaze lingered on Tad.

Tad seemed oblivious to the storm around him.

Manoah hid a smile. How had Samson, smaller than every other boy, captured them all? He was proud of him.

The room remained quiet.

Z'llpunith grabbed Tad from the basket and patted his back, obviously trying to calm herself and not the baby.

Manoah knew she wasn't happy. She pierced Manoah then Samson with her gaze, then broke the silence. "What have you to say for yourself?"

Samson looked between his parents. His eyebrows lifted in question. "I tried to play nicely, *Ima*. But they touched my hair."

Her voice rose several pitches. "You fought over your hair?"

Samson looked down.

Z'llpunith looked from Manoah to Samson. When she spoke again, she seemed more resigned than confident. "Samson, your anger is going to get you into trouble if you don't learn to control it."

She glared at Manoah and walked from the house, leaving Manoah alone with Samson.

Manoah watched her go. Was that look for him to do something? What was he to say that she hadn't already?

Quietness followed her departure.

Manoah squeezed Samson's shoulder. "Is it so hard to play with the others?"

Samson looked into his face. "They didn't include me."

Manoah nodded. "Is it so hard to be alone?"

"I like it. I don't have to do things their way."

Manoah wrinkled his forehead, hoping the silence would teach what he did not know. "Is their way so bad?"

Samson shrugged. "When their way doesn't work, why keep doing it the same way? They do not change, yet wonder why it fails."

"But don't you *want* to play with others?"

Samson shook his head. "No."

What could he teach about being alone? Their community was established by responsibility and accountability with others, not by isolated existence. How could this help Samson deliver their people if he couldn't even be with them now?

Before he could say anything more, Samson said, "He started it."

"He's your cousin. You don't want to hurt him."

"Yeah, I did."

Manoah tried another way, "Your anger gives you power."

Samson smiled. "He got two black eyes. I only have one."

Manoah stroked his beard and softened his voice, "Acting in anger will take away your ability to reason. You will do things you'll regret later."

Samson's eyebrows scrunched. "Does that mean I should let them win?"

Manoah sighed. "Sometimes when rage *controls* you, *you* do not win."

"Because I fight with myself and the "bad self" wins?"

Manoah nodded.

"How do you know if it's my "bad self" when I'm angry?"

Manoah squeezed his shoulder again. "Ask God. He will show you when your rage is right."

· · ·

The sun had only half risen in the sky when Z'llpunith reached Manoah's pastures. She breathed heavily from running, but she still mustered enough air to yell across the field, "Manoah, have you seen Samson?"

Manoah waited until she had reached him. "I last saw him this morning when we ate." Manoah offered his water skin for Z'llpunith to drink. "Don't fret about him."

Z'llpunith slowed her breathing to drink deeply. She wiped her lips. "I wouldn't worry if he played with other boys. But he stays by himself. Think what would happen if the Philistines found him in these hills."

Manoah's expression changed. "I'll speak to him."

Z'llpunith nodded. "That doesn't help me now."

"He'll come home to eat."

Z'llpunith sighed. "If he remembers."

She started to turn away, but Manoah grabbed her arm. "Z." He paused until she looked him in the eye. "I'm more concerned about you."

"Me?"

Manoah gestured to the other herdsmen scattered over the mountains.

"Your voice travels."

She looked at the other herdsmen.

They had dropped their heads conspicuously, as if they hadn't heard her hysterical screaming.

She lowered her head, embarrassed to be corrected. Her face felt hot. "Sorry, Manoah. I'm just concerned."

Manoah relaxed his grip and bent to kiss her. "I know, Z. Our boy's fine. God's preparing him for His mission."

Z'llpunith's eyes filled with tears. "Is he also preparing me for when he leaves us?"

Manoah hugged her. "He has not left us yet. Enjoy what time we're given."

Z'llpunith felt the soft leather of Manoah's cloak against her face. She could smell his man smell and the smells of his sheep and goats.

Those smells always brought comfort. She pulled away and wiped her eyes. "I feel like he's already left us."

Manoah rested his head against hers. "Then we'll enjoy the memories."

M anoah nodded to Samson that night after they had finished eating. "Come with me."

They both walked from the house to the edge of the fields.

The sun was setting and the evening chorus of frogs singing from the woods beyond the fields. Peace settled over the land. Even the Philistine threat seemed muted by the closing of the day.

They stood in silence, watching the night's sky shift from reds and oranges to deep blue.

"Look, *Abba!*" Samson pointed. "See the fox at the edge of the field where the wheat moves?"

Manoah squinted. "I hope he gets those mice eating my grain."

They watched the wheat move.

Manoah shoved his hands into his cloak's pockets and swallowed.

"I've a question for you, *Abba.*" Samson already had his distractions.

Manoah was relieved for the delay.

"Camels are unclean in our law. And so the milk from a camel is unclean. Correct?"

Manoah was pleased he was paying attention to the Law. Sometimes he wondered if Samson cared about any rules. "Yes."

"And bees are insects that don't hop, and so they are unclean; so why isn't honey unclean?"

Manoah sighed inwardly. This was another exception to show how illogical the Law was. "Samson, I don't understand the why's behind all the laws. But it's good we're allowed honey, isn't it?"

"Yes. But the laws seem—"

"Samson, you avoid obeying the Law. You want to walk as close to the edge of the cliff as you can without falling off."

"I like to see the view."

Manoah took a step away from Samson. "The view you will see is the dirt where your face lands. Desire to be close to God. He will show you a view more wondrous than you can imagine, but it will still lie within His Holy Law."

Samson bowed his head. "Yes, *Abba*."

Samson showed the outward signs of obedience and respect, but inwardly, Manoah knew, Samson didn't believe. Manoah sighed. "You try to understand God. And that's good. But God is so much bigger than you or me. If you could understand why He makes all these rules, then He wouldn't be very big. He could be understood. We have a God Who is above our comprehension. We can't understand all that He does. Understand?"

Samson nodded. "If I understood God, then I'd have nothing to learn about later."

Manoah smiled. "Right." Now about that other issue. He sighed. "Your *ima*'s concerned about you. What do you do during the day?"

Samson's voice grew animated as he told of exploring caves and finding animals' nests.

"Your *ima* worries about the Philistines."

Samson responded confidently, "I'd see them before they'd see me."

"But you're alone."

"No, I'm not." Samson shifted on his feet, suddenly unsure of himself.

Manoah studied Samson in the growing darkness. His words seemed defensive, then hesitant, as if he'd said too much. What was he hiding? "None of the village boys are with you."

Samson shrugged and kicked at a rock. "Those boys think only of what was done before, not what could be done now."

"How so?"

"Look at my slingshot." He took from his cloak pocket a hardened stick, stripped of bark and smoothed soft.

Manoah took the offered weapon, stretched the leather throngs back and released it. "It's balanced well. What do you shoot?"

Samson thrust back his shoulders. "I've shot a crowned sand grouse."

The bird blended into the desert and walked miles to carry water for its young.

Manoah arched his eyebrows. "Impressive." He felt the weight of the leather strip on the slingshot. "Why didn't your *ima* cook it?"

Samson hung his head. "I gave it to another."

"So, who's with you?" Manoah brought the subject back.

Samson looked up. His eyes pleading. "You won't tell *Ima*, will you?"

"You know, I can't keep secrets from *Ima*." Manoah squeezed Samson's shoulder.

"I don't want to upset her." Samson looked up and scrunched his forehead. "She'd worry."

"That's what *ima*'s do. But you still haven't told me who's with you."

Samson lowered his head and mumbled. "A dog."

"What?" Manoah knew there were no tame dogs in the village, nor would there be, as they were unclean and not permitted. Not even to touch them.

The earlier questions about unclean things now made sense. When would Samson learn to live by the Law rather than stretch the Law to fit how he wanted to live?

Samson looked into Manoah's face. His eyes sparkled with excitement, yet begged for acceptance at the same time. "I've . . . tamed a wild dog."

"Samson, your *ima* and I have raised you as a Nazirite." Manoah stopped, considering carefully his next words. He registered what Samson had said. A wild dog would be equal to a wolf in its tameness. "How tame is this dog?"

Samson's shoulders relaxed, as if he had been waiting for his father to accept his idea. "He comes when I whistle for him."

Manoah's own shoulders relaxed. At least the dog wouldn't attack him when he turned his back. "Why did you tame him?"

"Because I can."

Manoah measured the boy as he stood there. He was small for his age, but his agility made roaming the hills, forest, and riverbeds a need, not a want. "How did you do it?"

"I baited the dog with stuff I shot with my slingshot so he'd come to me."

Manoah hid his surprise. Shooting anything with a slingshot at Samson's age was nothing short of a miracle, but shooting enough to bait a dog—he shook his head.

How could he take away what Samson had worked so hard to achieve? Manoah chewed his lip as he thought.

"I respect the Nazirite vow. I don't eat the dog. He's only a companion." He was working hard to convince his father. "And he protected me from the horned viper."

Manoah raised his eyebrows. "Tell me."

Samson swallowed, realizing he had said too much again, but could no longer avoid telling the story. "We were walking together when the dog nearly attacked my foot."

"Samson, he's still wild. Wild animals shouldn't be tamed."

"But *Abba*, he wasn't attacking my foot. I almost stepped on the viper's horns. If the dog hadn't interrupted my step, I'd be dead."

There was no mistaking his sincerity, nor the danger. The venomous viper hid with only its horns exposed above the sand, waiting for its prey.

Samson seemed desperate now as he'd exposed his projects. "You won't tell *Ima*, will you?" He paused, shrugging his shoulders and smiling. "She'd only worry."

Manoah sighed. "She has a right to worry. Samson—"

"Please *Abba*, don't make me stop. I don't like being with the village boys. They want to grow up and accept slavery. They live like they're already defeated, not just by the Philistines but by life. I want to live life. I want to be a victor. I want to win." He said it with such passion, such heart.

Manoah tried to remember to shut his mouth. Was this the Lord preparing his son for His mission? His wife wasn't wrong about their son leaving them too soon. He swallowed the lump in his throat.

Manoah dug in his cloak's pocket for his knife. He handed it to Samson. "You keep this with you always. If that dog attacks you, do not hesitate. Use it."

"*Abba*, he would never—"

Manoah's voice was sharp and stern. A voice he hardly ever used with Samson. "Use it."

Samson lowered his head. "Yes, *Abba*."

"And Samson," Manoah waited until he had his son's undivided attention. "Your Nazirite vow is sacred. It is by your obedience to it that God will use you. I don't know how you can honor the vow with a dog, but you must decide how much you value God's help."

Samson answered with his characteristic confidence, yet enough humility to endear Manoah to him, "But didn't God bring the dog to me for my protection?"

Manoah shook his head. "I understand your need for protection, but God doesn't contradict His Word."

"But *Abba*, didn't God create the dog, just as He made the Philistine."

"Of course." Here was another law Samson hoped to change by twisting logic.

"And didn't He make all things good?"

"Son, you know our Law. The Philistine is worse than a dog when he refuses to acknowledge his Creator. And the dog returns to his own vomit after eating the dead. The next thing you're going to tell me is that you have a Philistine friend in the hills." The thought made him stop short and he looked sharply at Samson.

For once, Samson said nothing.

His silence made Manoah study him more closely. The darkness hid his features.

Did he want to know if Samson had a Philistine friend? Manoah shook his head. Parenting was harder than he had ever thought possible. "We'll not talk any more of this tonight."

As they made their way back to the house, Manoah's thoughts were more troubled than when they had left. How should he prepare his son for God's mission when he couldn't even convince him to obey the vow commanded before his birth? How should he have handled this?

There was no one he could ask, except God.

But God wasn't telling.

. . .

Z'llpunith waited until Samson was asleep before she turned to Manoah. "How did the talk go?"

"Fine." Manoah rolled on his back.

Z'llpunith could see by the moonlight that streamed through their window he was staring at the ceiling. She tried not to hurry him. "What did he say?"

"Samson asked if the camel and its milk is unclean, why isn't the bee's honey unclean."

"A question that's bothered me, too. But I'd hate to give up honey if that was declared unclean. What did you tell him?"

"I don't know. But my concern is Samson knows the Law so he can be as close to not breaking it as he can. Like a man standing at the edge of a cliff without plunging over."

Z'llpunith sat and leaned toward Manoah. "He thrives with a challenge with risks, even danger. He thinks safe is a boring existence. Should we curb that danger? Or make him safe within it?"

"I told him God's view of the cliff is beyond his expectations."

Z'llpunith kissed Manoah. "Good answer. Samson is not like everyone else. His birth ... His purpose ... But it scares me where it will take him. If we don't know how God will use him, how do we keep him safe?

Manoah twirled a strand of Z'llpunith's hair that had fallen lose from her braid. "We don't keep him safe. We give him for God's use. When God prepares a man, he protects him."

Z'llpunith's voice broke, "So we let him run wild by himself?"

"He's not by himself when God is protecting him."

"How?"

Manoah smiled. "I know where Samson gets his questions. Do you train him when I'm in the fields?"

Z'llpunith laughed, "Do not try to distract me, Manoah. How is he in danger?"

"Samson is fine."

"You aren't telling me something.

Manoah raised on his elbow to kiss her. "We commit Samson into God's hands and allow God to protect him in His way."

Z'llpunith said nothing more, but she knew Manoah wasn't telling her everything.

S amson looked for predator overhangs that he should watch when he moved the flocks. He noticed movement on the trail below him. The movement was more than just an animal—horses.

His wolf-dog at his feet bristled, its hair standing up on its neck. It emitted a low throat growl.

"Shhh Wolf. Not now." Samson warned. He watched a moment longer, then ran toward his village.

The Philistines would raid.

He kept to the high paths where they would not see him, but paralleled their movement, hoping the stream would slow them down so he could come down from the higher way and reach his village in time.

His need lent speed to his feet. His wolf-dog ran easily by his side.

He reached the place where he must finally make his way to the valley. The way was steep. He paused to jump from rock to outcrop. Each jump could be seen from below if they happened to glance up on the hill. He adjusted his tunic so it wouldn't catch on anything, then jumped.

When he reached the valley, he glanced back to where the Philistines were stopped at the stream. He would have only moments to warn his people. He turned and ran.

It was then he noticed Wolf was not at his side. He took a backward glance, before seeing Wolf poised on the path.

"Come, Wolf." Samson hissed through his teeth, so as not to alert the Philistine horses.

He saw their ears lift, but no Philistines seemed to notice.

Wolf did not move. His hackles were raised, and he stood firm as if guarding the path for Samson.

Samson could not wait. He ran.

He circled the hill of his own house, shouting, "Raiders are coming!"

His *abba* raised his arm in acknowledgement and ran to the barn to make sure all was hidden.

Samson kept running to the village. Arriving, he shouted through the one street, "The Philistines are coming!"

Several studied his face, as if to measure his words.

Why should he waste his time warning them if they did not believe him?

His cousin Ahiezer taunted, "If you're our deliverer, why don't you stop them before they come?"

"If you're man enough, why don't you stand with me and fight? Samson responded.

Ahiezer spit at him. "You're the one with the hovering angel. You protect us."

Down the street, doors slammed as others wasted no time in hiding their own.

The Philistines galloped through the street—ten of them.

His cousin glared once more at Samson, before shutting the door.

Why didn't his own people stand against them? If every man, able to fight would stand together, they could easily conquer these raiders!

When he had asked his *abba*, his *abba* had shaken his head, a gesture Samson recognized as frustration—at least when it was used towards him. "Fear. The people fear more what the Philistines will do than what God will do when we disobey. If these Philistines do not return, their families hold revenge as a great virtue."

Samson said, "But even if they do come in great numbers, our God is so much more powerful—"

Abba pursed his lips. "Our people forget God and seek their own pleasures. When danger comes, they do not remember that God is even there."

Samson nodded, but he did not understand.

Now Samson reflexively fingered for his dog's head at his side. When he did not feel him, he remembered Wolf would not enter the village.

Retracing his steps, Samson's anxiety increased. He whistled.

No response.

Samson circled back, past his family's house.

Why had Wolf not returned to him yet?

He had almost reached the path where they had parted when he saw a lump in the path that was not there before.

His heart jolted, and he swallowed before running faster.

A breeze blew.

Fur rose from the lump, stirred by the breeze.

An arrow, pointing toward the sky, lodged in the mound.

Samson groaned, his feet almost stopping.

He covered the remaining distance in dread.

Not one, but three arrows protruded through Wolf's chest. A pool of blood puddled beneath him.

A breeze lifted the fur on his back in a wave, only to allow it to settle back again.

Samson fell on his knees before the mound. "Wolf."

Samson grabbed one of the arrows to remove it, but Wolf licked Samson's fingers.

Withdrawing the arrow would make him bleed more.

Wolf was dying.

And Samson could nothing.

Tears coursed down his face. He licked his lips and tasted salt.

He could see where the horses had gone around him, off the path. Wolf had stood his ground, not letting the Philistines pass.

Until they shot him.

Samson scratched behind Wolf's ears. "You did good, boy."

But his own heart did not feel good. He had sacrificed his dog for his people who did not care.

CHAPTER 5

THREE YEARS LATER

As Samson helped his father with the herds, he wandered farther southeast than any others in their village. Not only were the pastures more plentiful because they were not used, but he yearned for the unknown. When there was a hill, he went to see what was on the other side. When there was a stream, he followed it to see where it started and ended. But it wasn't just his wonderment that drove him. He wanted life. Perhaps his boyhood days were leaving him, but his thirst for a challenge still drove him to go just a little farther.

He had been looking for a shearling. His father had admonished him to break its leg and carry it as it healed to curb its wandering lust, but he couldn't do it. He understood its need to see over the next horizon.

His father understood his need for what was wild, too. They both understood tending sheep was a ruse to allow him to do what he wanted.

His wandering hadn't been for naught. When the Philistines came, he had alerted the village several times, saving their herds and grain. Families hid those they valued in caves or underground rooms, preventing the Philistines from stealing their young girls.

But with freedom came responsibility. Samson resented his parents' reminders of what he had been born to do. Their nagging drove him to become wilder.

He knew the Law, even though many his age had forsaken it. His father said that was why the Philistines invaded—because their people had forgotten God. But was forgetting God equal to disobeying God?

Samson had reached the crest of another hill when he glimpsed movement in the ravine. Would his shearling have ventured that far? But careful watching showed it wasn't caused by an animal.

Even the birds had stopped singing.

Everything was quiet.

Sweat gathered on his forehead. He restrained from wiping it. The movement would attract attention from below.

He considered his terrain as he crawled back from the ridge.

A deer trail would bring him to where the movement was.

Samson took it, stepping noiselessly, his movements undetected from below because of the trees and bushes.

He stepped off the trail and crept toward the movement.

A lad, about his own age, crouched beneath a tree, his attention on the ground where dirt was freshly dug.

The boy was alone.

Samson spoke, "What are you doing?"

The youth jumped.

When he faced Samson, Samson noticed his tear-streaked face and blotchy, red eyes.

The Philistine (for his distinguished nose and prominent forehead gave him away) wiped his nose with his hand and stepped under the tree's shadows.

"I mean you no harm." Samson gestured toward the ground. "Need help?"

Instead of responding, the lad bolted down the trail.

Samson ran after him, his short legs taking two strides to cover the other's long one. They dodged fallen logs, ducked under low-hanging branches, and jumped the stream at the bottom of the hill with matched agility.

As Samson became winded from pursuing, the other seemed finally to slow down as well.

Trees and brushes thinned. The path stretched before them.

Samson gathered his strength and jumped, landing on the Philistine's back.

They both tumbled, rolling some distance before untangling themselves.

They sprang to their feet and faced each other, both breathing deeply.

The sadness was gone from the youth's eyes, and now they flashed a challenge. "I've met my match."

Samson liked the sparkle in his eye. He nodded. No one in his village could ever keep up with him, let alone maneuver the hills. Here was one who could.

"Escaped from the Egyptians? Still running, but this time toward people."

Samson lifted his eyebrows. A fitting description of his people, who *had* escaped from Egypt, leaving culture and people behind to wander, it seemed, for forty years in the wilderness. Here was a youth, his own age, who spoke his mind. Samson smiled. "Samson, from Zorah."

The youth nodded. "Lucas, from Timnah."

"A Philistine. Known for your wild ways."

"Me, wild? It wasn't me who crept on one grieving."

"Yes, about that—sorry." Samson lowered his head. "Grieving about what?"

Lucas's face changed as he swallowed. He seemed embarrassed to speak of it. He shrugged as if it meant nothing now. "My dog."

Samson remembered his boyhood dog. His friendly banter was gone, in its place genuine sadness. "I'm sorry."

Lucas tone grew defensive. "How would you know? Jews don't even own dogs."

"I did. I tamed a wild one. He alerted me of danger." Samson smiled, "Of your people coming."

Lucas looked around. "Where's it now?"

Samson nodded toward Timnah. "Your scout didn't like it when it barked and warned of their coming. He shot it with an arrow." He swallowed and looked away.

Lucas shook his head. "My people have a way of making enemies."

Samson shrugged. Lucas was not like the other Philistines—coming to plunder his people—but a kindred spirit. Samson extended his arm.

Lucas took it.

They embraced. And returned to bury Lucas's dog.

Shared grief unites when nothing else can.

And so, their friendship grew, advancing God's plan for saving His people.

O n this morning, Samson continued far beyond where his father's flocks pastured. He watched to the west for any movement on the trail below him. He focused on the path, though his eyes could detect anything off the trail that moved.

He saw movement.

Feeling in his pocket for the right size stone, he placed it in his sling. He flexed his fingers and tensed his arm as he watched for the right moment.

The moving leaves below were closer and not caused by any breeze.

It was not an animal.

He watched the opening in the trees where the sun's light reached the ground, tensed and waiting.

He saw the foot before the rest of the body.

He swung his arm and let the stone go.

The stone thudded when it landed, before he heard the grunt.

"How did you know I was here? I was quiet!" Lucas looked up the hill.

By his searching, Samson knew Lucas hadn't found him yet. He swung another stone, this time a cubit ahead of Lucas.

Lucas stepped back when it landed, still searching the hillside. "Where are you?"

Samson bounded down the hill to where Lucas was. "The quietness gave you away. I had only to watch for unexplained movement."

Lucas's shoulders sagged. "How do I make the birds sing?"

"You can't make them sing, but you mimic their song." Samson whistled a bird song. "Let's go to the stream." He led down the hill to where the stream still flowed, in spite of the dry season leaving everything else brown.

When they reached the stream, Samson watched the water for a few moments, before drinking.

The stream wasn't deep enough to swim, but it did offer coolness . . . and bugs.

Samson raised his cloak over his head, to keep the flies from biting him and settled against the trunk of a tree. "You mimic the birds."

Samson laughed at Lucas's raised eyebrows. "Like this—" He whistled a short clip that sounded like a bird. "Or this." He made another bird's chirp, "Then I won't know you are coming."

Lucas plopped on the ground, letting his feet dangle in the water. He laid back, his arms under his head and puckered his lips.

Lucas's whistle pierced the air like an alarm.

Samson laughed. "Open your lips more, and don't blow out so much air at one time."

Lucas yanked a grass stem and chewed on it, rather than try to whistle again. "How do you know all this?"

Samson shrugged. "I watch. And listen. I'm alone a lot."

"I am, too. But—"

"How can you be alone in a city?"

Lucas laughed. "There's a lot of people, but no one cares what you're doing. You could shout in the streets and no one would listen." Lucas looked sideways at Samson, "Unless you yelled, 'Fire!'"

"Sounds like you've done that before."

Lucas shrugged. "It was worth the beating."

Samson laughed. "Yea, my *abba* would have something to give me, too."

"My father didn't care. It was the leaders who gave it to me."

"Why?"

"The leaders are responsible to make the city safe."

"But doesn't your father make you obey?"

Lucas raised his eyebrows. "Does your father *make* you obey?"

Samson laughed, "Well, no. But he cares enough to make sure I won't think to do *that* again."

Lucas shook his head. "Your father cares that much?"

Samson couldn't understand his question. "Why wouldn't he?"

Lucas studied Samson with longing. "I do anything I want."

"But isn't that great?" Samson egged him on. "No rules bind you."

Lucas responded sarcastically. "Sure. No rules is great." He took his feet out of the water and sat up. "I know what we can do. Why don't we go to your house?"

Samson wrinkled his forehead. "Why?"

Lucas's eyes danced. "I don't know. I've never met your father." He paused, thinking. "Or your mother."

Samson shook his head. "I don't think that's a good idea."

"Why?"

"Your people aren't exactly looked with favored in our community."

Lucas's excitement faded. "Oh, yeah."

Samson shrugged, "Our friendship wouldn't be accepted well, either."

Lucas sighed. "Would you get a beating?"

Samson hesitated. "My *abba* understands my need to be different from the community. But he may not understand a Philistine friendship." He shrugged. "My *ima* would *not* be so understanding."

Lucas leaned back on the dirt again. His excitement gone.

Samson whistled a few bird songs absently. What would his parents do if they even knew about his friendship? Did he want to know?

A fish splashed in the spring.

"Let's trap it."

Lucas sat again and collected the branches needed to weave a net.

Samson breathed a sigh of relief. Lucas had so wanted to go to his house. He hated to deny him, but he was a Philistine after all. And what would his *abba* say if he knew how much time he spent with Lucas?

Not that Lucas was bad, but their people lumped all Philistines together as wicked.

Lucas was nothing of the kind. In fact, Lucas was his only friend.

CHAPTER 6

TEN YEARS LATER

S amson hiked the hills, tracking the mountain lion that had killed ten of their lambs. Soon they'd only have the old ewes who were too tough to eat but too old to breed. He hitched his belt more tightly around his waist and raised his water skin to drink.

He followed the river valley. The tracks led up, probably to the lion's lair. It should be full after feasting on lamb. But Samson could not be certain.

Mountain lions loved nothing more than to watch their prey before leaping.

He studied the mountain before ascending, listening. Birds would tell him by their silence if something was wrong.

He reached the crest of the mountain and studied the view below.

The Philistines' fields and vineyards covered the fertile plains and hillsides of the mountains to the east and south of their city.

He thought he had hiked all over these mountains, but this view was new to him. He felt drawn to it. Like a thirst that wouldn't be satisfied until he had drunk his fill.

S amson swallowed his flatbread and pushed back from the table. He rubbed Tad's head and sighed contentedly. "Good meal, *Ima*."

Tad pushed away. "Don't touch my hair."

Samson laughed. "Sounds familiar."

His mother raised her eyebrows, "Then you should respect your brother's wishes."

Samson laughed.

Manoah leaned forward, holding his tea. "Looks like you have something on your mind, Samson."

His mother poured his tea. "He has ever since he went after that lion."

Samson laughed. "If I could read his tracks like you read my mind, *Ima*, I'd have found that lion."

"Do not try to distract." She pushed the platter of matzo layered with fig spread in front of him.

Samson took a generous bite. His father would understand his need to pursue this challenge. But he steeled himself against his *ima*'s reaction. "I'm leaving."

Tad asked, "Can I go, too?"

Samson rubbed his head again, "You don't even know where I'm going."

Tad countered, "Neither do you."

Samson laughed. "Not this time. You have herds to watch."

"What about your herds?"

Samson jerked his head at their father. "They are *Abba's*, not mine."

His mother bit her lip as she always did when she was trying not to cry.

Manoah sipped his tea, seeming unaware of the disruptions around him. But Samson knew better. His father was always slow to speak, but Samson could hardly wait to shake the words from his lips now.

When his father raised his head to meet Samson's gaze, he gave a slight nod. It told him enough. He understood. No words were needed.

S amson traveled west, over the mountains beyond his boyhood wanderings. He followed deer trails to the valley where a stream flowed when the rains came. He refilled his water skin and swatted a fly biting his neck. Covering his head with his hood, he exposed less skin for insects to chew, but it hindered him from hearing as well. He carried a blanket at the insistence of his *ima*, strapped on his back with a belt his *abba* gave. Even Tad had wanted to give him something. He handed him a stone he could use for protection. He added it to those in his pocket gathered from the riverbed. His slingshot, made better than his boyhood one of long ago, stayed ready in his pocket. Deeper in his pocket, he still carried his father's knife. He had never used it against his dog, but it had been handy had many times for hunting his dog's food.

Thinking of his dog led him to think of Lukas. Would he find him?

Sunshine streamed through the leaves where less underbrush covered the ground. Beyond the trees, the valley opened up.

Vineyards crept up the hillsides making use of the lingering sunlight. It was the season when grapes needed the sweet lick of sunshine to turn their skins from green to dark purple.

Wheat stood in fields the color of rich green. It would be ripe in a few more cycles of the moon. Dirt pathways crossed between them, allowing carts to retrieve produce at the end of rows.

Beyond the seemingly endless fields stood the city. He had expected a village like his own. Never had Samson seen such a city! It could hold more people than he had ever seen at one time.

He quickened his pace, walking through the vineyards. He startled a fox from the weeds below the vines. It bolted and ran toward the trees. He watched it go.

What a bold thing to be out during the day! Or hungry.

When he reached the valley, he stood at the edge of a wheat field. The kernels would not be ripe until the stalks had turned the color of dry sand.

Rather than take the pathways around the field, he walked boldly through the field. He wished the wheat were ripe. If it were, the kernels would fall to the ground with each step.

He could feel why the Philistines did this to his own village. It gave a sense of power. Ownership. And for him, revenge. But because the wheat was not ready, the kernels clung to the stalks, and even the stalks he walked on quickly stood back up after his departure.

Soon the Philistines would be coming to his village. Their harvest would again be destroyed. But their harvest was nothing like this. These fields looked well cared for, as if a gardener carefully tended them, not like his own people who must watch over their shoulder at every passing cloud to see if a Philistine were coming.

What freedom this city had!

He looked beyond the fields.

Before he even reached the city walls, he could see that a great crowd was gathered. Sheep, goats, horses, cows, and chickens were corralled in pens, surrounded by people gesturing and haggling over prices.

Samson was curious about one animal. It was low to the ground, on short legs, barely large enough to carry its huge body. Its short tail curled almost in a knot. He looked over the pen full of these animals. Some had tusks that looked more like a weapon for a warrior; not like something for an animal people would herd. They did not have fur, but dark skin with coarse hair. One rubbed against the wooden planks of the fence where he stood.

After scratching, the animal snorted and began rooting in the dirt, furrowing deep holes.

Samson leaned on the corral fence and nodded toward a man beside him. "What are those?"

The man looked him over, his gaze lingering on Samson's hair. "What are you? One of those foreigners who don't eat pigs?"

Samson looked back at the animals. So these were pigs. He hid his anger at the stranger's slur by smiling. "With a smell like that, it's good to avoid such an animal."

The man responded in defense. "The smell is forgotten when its meat melts in your mouth with spicy sauces and smoked flavors." He said it with such pleasure Samson was reminded of his hunger.

Samson walked toward the city gate. Mooing, bleating, and grunting were left behind. In their place, merchants called over the steady mumble of voices as the quiet wilderness was left behind. Leaving the odors of hay and animals, Samson followed his nose to the smells of food ahead.

In his village everyone knew his business; here people did not even glance at him. They kept their eyes down even as they passed. And no one smiled.

The market stalls changed from boarded corrals to those made of stone with thatched roofs. Their produce sprawled over tables, hung on hooks, attached to walls, and overflowed on blankets spread in front of the stalls. Everything imaginable was sold—spices, vegetables, tools, leather work, silks. He could spend weeks looking.

"You, with the long hair."

Samson saw a man gesturing for him to come closer.

The merchant pointed to a bed of coals, smoldering behind him. He pulled a stick from the embers, the meat on the other end still smoking. "Try."

Samson smelled rosemary, onions, garlic, and something he could not identify. He licked his lips. His mouth watered. He hesitantly bit into the meat. Juice exploded in his mouth. The meat was nothing like he had ever tasted. "This is good."

The merchant held out his hand for payment.

Samson patted his pocket. He hadn't thought of payment.

The man had just given it to him.

He had nothing of value in his pockets.

The man gestured to the leather-tooled belt he used to wrap his blanket.

Samson removed the belt with hesitation. His father had made it. It was worth more than a piece of meat.

The merchant examined the leather's softness and design. "Where did you get this?"

His father would tool such things regularly if the Philistines would allow him to keep his hides. Samson shrugged, rather than answer him.

The man studied him a moment. He gestured toward the coals. "Take two."

Samson was hungry. He hadn't eaten anything all day, nor much the last few days, as game had been scarce. Each stick held a hearty amount of meat, interspersed with vegetables. He shook his head. "I will have four."

The merchant gestured to the coals, dismissing him as he directed his attention to another possible customer.

As Samson grabbed the sticks, he realized he had let his hunger control him. He should have bartered for more. His belt was worth more. A whole lot more.

He chewed slowly, marveling at its flavor. Juices dripped down the stick and over his hands. The meat was tender. Before he realized it, he had finished them all. After licking his fingers, he wiped them on his cloak.

Now that his belly was full, he yawned. If he were in the wilderness, he would find a cave to take a nap, content with his full stomach. But another merchant beckoned him. "You with the long hair."

Samson looked around. Even though not as tall as others, his hair made him stand out. Most man were shaved almost bald. Was he the only one with long hair?

He approached the stall. Knives covered a table. Daggers and longer blades hung behind the man's head. Their blades sparkled as sunlight hit them.

His people had nothing but what they could hew from rocks. He had never considered where his father had gotten the knife he had given Samson so long ago.

Now Samson hefted one knife in his hand. The balance and weight of its handle were perfect. How much easier would it be to work, if all his people were allowed these knives.

Samson wanted it more than anything he had ever wanted before.

What could he barter? He should have waited to eat and used his leather belt for this. His blanket hung wadded up and tied by leather strings to his back since he had removed the leather belt. His *ima* wove blankets prized by those in his village as the best. He unfastened the strings and spread it over the table of knives for the merchant to examine. Samson tried not to think how cold he would be on his return home without the blanket.

The merchant's eyes widened.

Samson motioned for the dagger behind the man.

As the man turned, Samson slipped the knife into his pocket. He had been cheated by the first merchant, and he would not be cheated by another. He had learned quickly that honesty did not fill stomachs nor protect his property.

The man handed him the dagger.

Its weight surprised him. The metal was solid. The blade sharp.

He gestured to another one. "I'll have two."

The man's eyes narrowed, but he handed Samson another one from a different place on his display.

Samson tested the second one. The metal seemed lighter, the handle inferior. He pointed to where the man had taken the first dagger. "One of those."

The man's shoulders slumped, but he reached for another.

Samson turned the new one in his hand and nodded. "I'll take this." He strapped both on his belt and walked away.

In the background, Samson heard. "Thief! He took my knife!"

Turning down another aisle, Samson drifted into the crowd. He felt no remorse for the extra knife he had acquired. It was part of the barter.

When he reached the city wall, he stopped. From a distance, the size could not be measured. Nothing he had ever seen compared to the size and structure. Imagine the safety of those who lived within the walls!

Farmers, merchants, and travelers pushed him to keep moving.

The people energized him. The newness of everything challenged him. He no longer felt tired but alert and alive.

Passing the gate, he glanced at its height. Two men could stand on top of one another and still not touch the top! And the walls that encased the gate were three cubits deep. His people would feel safe in walls like these!

Just inside the gates, the area opened up. Sunshine poured over all the people. Men sat on benches before a speaker.

Samson strained to hear what they were saying, but the crowd pushed him down a street.

Everyone seemed to know where they were going. Everyone but him. Doors opened and closed on either side of the street as people went about their business.

Buildings rose on either side of street, blocking the sun.

He felt restricted, unable to breathe.

The constant, loud noise made it hard for him to think.

He broke from the crowd onto a quieter street. It narrowed more like a path. Only a few walked here.

Could this many people live so close together in peace?

As if in answer, yelling erupted.

He paused by an open doorway.

A woman beat a child.

Should he intervene? He continued on, watching the people instead of his path. And veered to the middle of the street. Slop squished between his toes. Flies swarmed from human waste, rotten food and unidentified mush.

He moved from the center of the street. He would do better to watch where he was going.

He scraped his sandals against one of the raised cobblestones and wiped his hand down his cloak as if he could wipe the filth from him.

A rat slunk beside him into a dark crack in the wall. Beside the crack a figure sat. Was it human?

It was. His head rested on his knees at a grotesque angle. His arms circled his knees. His eyes held a haunted, vacant look.

Samson shivered and looked away. Did they leave their own to die in the street?

Farther down the street, light penetrated.

Samson hurried toward it.

Here the street widened.

Houses were set back from the streets, lined with walls. Figs, dates, and fruit trees hung over walls.

Their blossoms' smells cleared Samson's nose of the street's filth.

Laughter drifted over one wall. Or was it music?

It drew him.

He jumped to grab the top of the wall and pulled himself to sit on its top. He looked down into a courtyard.

A woman tossed a ball to a dog.

The dog was no bigger than his arm. It jumped and twisted to catch it before returning the ball to her.

The woman rewarded it with a chunk of meat.

The dog gulped it down and licked the woman's fingers.

Samson's gaze was drawn to the woman.

Her hair cascaded around her face and down her shoulders in ebony ringlets. Her skin was flawless and looked soft.

"You may come down from that wall."

Had she meant him? She had not looked his way.

Samson scrambled down.

"Come out of the shadows and let me see you."

Her boldness surprised him. His own people would not allow a woman to speak to a man without her father's presence.

Samson obeyed, stepping forward. They were alone, yet she showed no fear of a stranger, nor appeared bothered by his presence.

She was more beautiful than any woman he had ever seen.

"You're not from here."

Samson coughed to clear his throat. "No."

She laughed. "Nor do you explain yourself."

The dog tugged at the ball in her hand.

She ruffled the fur on its head. "Don't bother me anymore. I've something better to play with." She threw the ball.

The dog caught it and retreated beneath a bush, chewing on the rag ball, as if it had decided the game was over.

She tucked her bare feet under her tunic and patted the bench beside her. "Talk to me."

Samson shifted his water skin and daggers. He pushed his cloak behind him and sat on the edge of the bench. He smelled peach blossoms and honey.

She moved closer to him. The smell came from her.

She lowered her voice. "Tell me about yourself."

Before he could answer, she turned her dark eyes on him. He almost couldn't hear her next words for the deep liquid pools that sparkled there.

"Don't tell me you have nothing to say."

Was she like his *ima* who could read his thoughts? He fidgeted under her gaze.

The dog startled him by jumping on his lap.

She laughed. Her laughter was music even the birds stopped to hear. The woman rubbed the dog's ears. "You little traitor." She looked at Samson. "You *are* special. He doesn't go to anyone but me. Now I *must* know who you are."

Samson scratched the dog behind its ears as it scrambled for a comfortable spot. He shifted away from her to think better. He felt the loss, even as he did. He fingered the dog's leather collar, studded with gems, absentmindedly.

"I once had a dog. Well, I didn't have the dog. He had me. The dog guarded me. We roamed the hills as inseparable companions. My only sadness was leaving him behind whenever I went home."

"Why?"

He sighed. "He belonged to the mountains and I belonged to people."

"You sound like some wild man who doesn't like people."

"My people live like yesterday is all they have. I live for the future and what it will bring."

"You take risks. Not only are you a wild man, but also a brave man."

Her words encouraged him to tell more. He told how he roamed the hills, tamed his dog, and stalked mountain lions.

When he paused, the woman plied him with questions, encouraging him to continue. When he told how he met Lukas, she interrupted.

"Lukas?"

"I haven't seen him in quite a while. But he came from this city."

"He still lives here."

How would she know him? Before Samson could ask her, she redirected the conversation back to Samson. She listened with her heart.

He shared his dreams, his wants—things he'd never told another.

He paused, shifting his leg that had fallen asleep under the dog's weight.

The dog stretched and jumped from his lap. It twirled in circles under a bush before laying down with its head on its paws.

The woman's hand, that had rested on the dog, now rested on Samson's thigh.

He held her hand. It was soft and small in his. He felt complete with this woman, like life could not exist anymore without her.

A servant paused a few steps from where they sat. "Tia, your father wants you."

She looked toward the house, then back at him. "You will return?" She no longer commanded but asked.

He pushed a strand of hair from her face. "I will."

She smiled. "I will wait."

Samson watched her retreating form until she vanished through a door. He leaped over the wall and retraced his way from the city, whistling. He would have that woman for his wife.

But he had forgotten his people's law against marrying foreign women.

Z'llpunith peeled the last fig and dropped it in the bowl. She sprinkled a bit of honey to give it a spreadable texture and smashed the ripened fruit into paste. Manoah loved his fig spread. If they had nothing else, Z'llpunith made sure to have enough fig spread for him to spread lavishly across his flatbread or his matza or a slice of fruit.

The Lord had blessed them with Tad, the son of their old age. Was this the Lord's way to ease the pain of Samson's leaving?

It had been several moons since he had left. Still, she did her work, watching for his return.

When would Samson deliver their people? At his birth, others had been excited at the promise of deliverance. But as Samson grew, criticism of how he didn't follow their customs and fulfill their expectations brought condemnation rather than praise.

It was not for her to explain God's deliverance. But each time the Philistines attacked, she felt her people's rebuke. Soon the Philistines would return. Another year's harvest would be destroyed or stolen from them.

She glanced from her work. She knew that lanky silhouette anywhere.

Samson covered the distance with a confident stride. As he drew closer she noticed several hares hung from a string at his waist. He'd probably caught them in a trap or shot them with his slingshot, but he hadn't stopped to eat. He would be hungry, as always, from his return journey.

Where was his belt? She looked more closely. And where was his blanket?

As Z'llpunith watched, Tad ran to meet him. Samson swung him around in a hearty hug. They walked back together, their arms around each other's shoulders.

Samson swept into the doorway and engulfed her in a tight hug. He smelled of the woods and desert. His face lit with delight. "Figs!" He stuck his finger in the bowl and licked it.

She swatted his hand. "Wash your hands."

"*Ima*, I'm famished."

Z'llpunith laughed. It was as if he had never left.

Yet her heart told her it would never be like before.

S amson picked an onion from the pan and popped it into his mouth. "That's hot!"

Z'llpunith stirred the meat and vegetables again before moving it from the flames.

Samson attempted to take another.

She swatted his hand. "Not until your *abba* returns."

"I'll starve."

Manoah approached the door. "You will live to see another day." He washed his hands and face at the basin by the door. He greeted both sons with a hug, then settled before the meal and prayed.

"Wheat looks good, *Abba*."

Manoah nodded.

Tad sat beside Samson. "I saw a roe deer grazing with our sheep."

"A deer?" Samson's eyes twinkled. "And you didn't add it to our dinner?"

Tad looked down. "It was too small."

Samson laughed. "Or too fast for you?"

Tad shrugged. His face brightened. "I saw a fox snatch a chicken."

"And you didn't catch it?"

Tad again felt rebuked. "Didn't have my slingshot."

Samson corrected. "Always carry your slingshot."

Z'llpunith listened to their banter. Tad sought Samson's praise, not his correction. Did Samson know his influence on him? But now was not the time to tell him. Something had changed Samson. Or someone. Her heart lurched at the insight. Had he found someone? She studied him—the twinkle in his eyes, his light step, his giddy enthusiasm.

She lost her appetite and could hardly swallow. How could any foreign woman keep him true to his mission? She pushed her food from her, unable to eat.

Manoah finished his meal and stretched his legs.

Z'llpunith brought hot water for his tea, dropping mint leaves into his vessel. She moved to fix Samson's vessel.

"No, *Ima*. I don't need tea. But dinner was perfect. My own cooking can never compare."

She felt her cheeks blush. "When do you cook your meals?"

Samson laughed. "I don't cook unless I can help it. It takes too long. But dinner was great. Only I wish I could have had fig spread." His eyes twinkled.

She gasped. "I forgot to put it on the table."

Manoah added, "I wondered, but I didn't want to ask."

"You should have." She put the bowl before them with more flatbread.

Manoah leaned forward and swathed flatbread with a thick layer of the figs. He closed his eyes as he took his first bite, chewing a long time before swallowing. He looked at Z'llpunith. "That was worth the wait." Then he turned to Samson, "How was your trip?"

Samson smiled, then laughed. "*Abba*, you won't believe it. But—" He seemed unable to speak. Then he blurted out, "I've found a woman to marry."

Although Z'llpunith had guessed, she choked on her drink.

Tad grinned. "Is she pretty?"

Samson looked from his father to his mother. "There's not much to say. When I searched for that mountain lion and saw the hills to the west of us, I longed to know what was there. I didn't understand why . . . until I crossed through the valley and reached the city on the other side."

Z'llpunith interrupted, "A Philistine city."

Samson shrugged. "It was bigger than anything I'd ever seen. Merchants sold all sorts of wares: cooked meats, fruits, vegetables, tapestries, silks—they would look beautiful on you, *Ima*." He untied the string at his waist and removed one of his daggers. "I bought this for you, *Abba*."

Manoah's eyes widened. He tested the weight and balance. "Thank you, son."

"Is that why you don't have your belt or blanket?"

Samson's eyes widened. "Do you read my life like you read my mind, *Ima*? As a matter of fact, I traded both. The merchants were greatly impressed by their quality."

"Did you use the rock I gave you?" Tad interjected.

Samson dug in his cloak pocket and retrieved the stone. "I saved it until my life depends upon it." Samson reached over and ruffled Tad's hair

Tad moved away. "Stop it."

Samson turned to his *ima*. "Your blanket brought me two daggers." Samson gulped his water.

Z'llpunith tried to smile. But she could not forget where this was leading.

Samson would never survive the city. There were too many people.

"I stumbled down a street where I heard laughter. I followed it to a courtyard."

"Oh Samson, didn't you fear soldiers?"

"*Ima*, not everywhere is war and hardship."

She interjected, "Nor is it wild and free. You must think before you act."

Samson's light banter was gone. His voice held an edge. "Many times, if I thought first, I'd be dead."

Manoah squeezed her hand. "Let Samson tell his story."

Z'llpunith felt rebuked. Samson's impetuousness could cost him. Yet his response showed a distance from her that she didn't like.

Samson continued. "A woman played with a dog, but invited me to join her." He turned to Tad, "And yes, she was the most beautiful woman I've ever seen."

Tad laughed.

Z'llpunith spoke under her breath, "An unclean animal with a foreign woman."

Samson spoke louder. "I found myself telling her things I'd never shared with anyone before."

This woman was playing with Samson. How could Samson do God's mission living with those they despised?

Manoah squeezed her, then sat straighter. "What's her family like? What does her father do? What's her name?"

Samson smiled. His eyes took a distant look. "Tia. Her name is Tia."

Her name meant princess. She would demand much from Samson. Was he willing to give all that it would cost?

What kind of spell had this Philistine woman cast over him? Z'llpunith did not like this woman. She could only stare ahead and will her tears not to pool. She had already isolated Samson by speaking. She clamped her lips shut. She would wait until he rested and had time to reconsider.

He would see their wisdom.

Manoah coughed beside her, interrupting her internal battle.

She sighed. Samson would listen to his father's counsel.

Manoah took a sip from his vessel. "Perhaps we've been wrong to cater to your desire to be alone, your talent for hunting and tracking, even taming that dog. Perhaps I should have forbidden it. I couldn't understand how ignoring your own village could be God's plan to save our people. And now it has led to this."

Samson interrupted. "*Abba*, that is *not* what we're talking about."

Manoah lifted his hand to demand silence. His voice raised to a pitch never used to correct Samson. "Foreign wives led our people into bondage and sin."

Z'llpunith interjected. "Couldn't you find a woman in one of our neighboring villages?"

Manoah patted her hand, "Not now, Z."

Samson's face flushed. With great restraint, he answered, "Our women live in fear of the past. I live in hope for the future."

Z'llpunith interrupted, "They live in fear because Philistines come at any moment to steal their joy."

Manoah raised his hand again. "How can you save your people from the Philistines when you are married to one? Have you forgotten why you were born?"

Samson spit out the words as if they were bile. "How can I forget, when every waking moment you remind me? Can't you forget the angel of the Lord—who hasn't come in twenty-five years—and think about what I want?"

Manoah stood. His knuckles white as he clenched his fists. "For any happiness to come to you, you must submit to the Lord's way."

Samson punched the doorframe before turning back. "If your life of dreary existence and fear is any indication of that *hap-pi-ness* you want to *bless me with,* I don't want any part of it." He stomped out the door, strode through the wheat field, and disappeared over the hill without looking back.

Z'llpunith lay in bed before the light of the new day brought chores. She had gone to bed early but had tossed all night. It had been one day since Samson had left. All day she had watched for his return. She neglected her chores. She'd forgotten to cook, although Manoah had not eaten much either. Tad hovered around her as if to comfort.

This was not how she had imagined Samson's leaving.

Samson was a good son. He had taken away her barren curse. Hadn't the Lord promised to use him?

How wrong would marrying a foreign wife be?

She was torn between trying to make things right by Samson's choice and knowing the Law forbade foreign marriage, at least under these circumstances.

This woman, enticing her innocent son, would plunge a dagger in his heart. Z'llpunith hated her!

Manoah wrapped his arm around her.

She snuggled against him, burrowing her face against his shoulder. "Will he return?"

"He's our son."

His answer did not comfort.

"Samson forgets his life is not his own. God has not forgotten His plan. He can use even Samson's disobedience to deliver our people from bondage.

Z'llpunith pulled her covers closer around her, as if that would guard against the pain. "He's so impulsive—acting, then thinking. It'll get him killed in the city. And with this woman—"

Manoah shrugged. "Or keep him alive. We should support him in this decision."

Z'llpunith raised her voice, "You mean, allow him to marry this *dog*?"

"Do you want to see your son again? And your grandchildren? He'll marry the woman anyway, but then he may never come home. Is that what you want?"

"No, but—"

"There are no 'but's in Samson's mind." Manoah planned out loud. "He won't return, so we must go after him."

"Isn't that like going to the enemy's camp?"

"Do you want your son to return?"

Z'llpunith sighed. "When do we go?"

"He's one day ahead of us."

"Can we catch him?"

Manoah smiled. "He left behind his water skin. He's either very thirsty or wondering what to do at the edge of the woodlands."

"What will we do when we find him?"

"We'll know when we find him."

CHAPTER 7

When Samson had stalked away from his parents, he had no thought of return. He was finished with their restrictive laws. Done with their mission for his life. Let them keep their oppression that hung over everyone like a wet woven mat!

He only wished he had grabbed his water skin before leaving. He needed it to return to Timnah.

He knew his history. Wasn't Rahab a foreigner? Bringing foreign wives was common after battle, too. What difference was there?

He was too absorbed with his thoughts to notice his surroundings.

He did not hear the warning until he felt the uneasy quietness.

Then he felt watched.

His hair raised on the back of his neck.

Now every sense was alert.

He flexed his fingers, then fingered his dagger, lifting it from its sheath.

The great beast cast a long shadow as it leaped from the cliff above Samson just before it struck. Its impact slammed Samson to the ground.

Samson reacted by protecting his throat with his arms.

His head knocked against the ground.

His dagger flew from his hand.

The lion's claws grazed him, ripping his tunic, leaving ribbons of blood beading across his chest.

They rolled together, sliding down the hillside.

When they stopped, Samson disentangled himself from the lion, jumping to his feet.

Before the beast steadied for another attack, Samson jumped on its back. Wrapping his feet around its belly, he yanked its mane, snapping its head back.

The lion twisted and clawed but could not reach Samson. It snarled with angry defiance.

The surprise of the attack had worn off. Samson's head throbbed. Sweat dropped from his face. Blood from his chest wounds dripped through his slashed tunic and splashed on the lion's back. His muscles burned from the strain of holding the beast's head back.

How long could he hang on?

His fingers were slipping from their hold. His arms shook from the tension. As weariness spread through his body, helplessness crept into his heart.

Images of Tia and his family flashed through his mind.

His strength was gone.

His cramped legs loosened their hold.

His fingers could no longer hold the head back.

His arms throbbed with exhaustion.

He could not hold its head anymore.

The lion growled, sensing his weakening.

Samson could feel the lion's legs tense for another twist that would throw him off his back.

Samson's head fell forward. He knew he was finished.

Instantly a new strength poured through his chest, arms, legs and fingers. This strength was not his own.

Samson felt hope.

He inched his fingers forward, grabbing the lion's jaws and twisting upward.

The lion writhed under the pressure, growling low as air escaped its throat.

Samson held his own breath as the beast's hot, putrid breath poured over his face.

With a pop, the lion's jaw fell slack.

Samson repositioned his grasp, ready for another twist, but waited.

The beast stopped struggling.

With a tighter hold, he pulled the broken jaw up, twisting its neck, lifting its head.

A loud crack resounded.

The pressure against Samson's hands went slack.

The lion slumped and convulsed.

Samson held his breath.

No movement came from under him.

Had he broken its neck?

Was it dead?

Samson rested his head on the lion's mane and breathed.

He let go, one hand at a time, flexing his fingers.

He shook his arms. They tingled as pressure was relieved.

He rubbed his hands to bring feeling into them.

He stepped from the carcass. He stood on shaky legs.

And watched, expecting it to rise again.

It did not.

As he watched the big form, he shook, reliving the moment his strength had been spent.

His mouth was dry. He reached for his water skin, only to remember he had left it at home.

Death had been close. Too close.

Life was precious.

From where had his strength come?

He knew it hadn't come from him.

There was only one answer.

He sank to his knees, leaned on the carcass, and thanked God for sparing his life.

What better way to deliver a people than by first experiencing deliverance oneself?

He would never tell his *ima* about this one. His quick response had initially saved him, but only God's strength had kept him alive. Would *Abba* believe his story?

Tia came to mind. He smiled. Now, this would be a story to tell her.

L eaving the lion on the hillside, Samson stumbled to the nearest stream. He drank deeply, allowing the coolness to soothe his throat. Taking his time, he washed his tunic. His blood colored the water as he shook it under the water's ripples. After spreading the tunic on a nearby bush, he searched the sides of the stream for comfrey. Resembling a shrub, its dark leaves contrasted with the tender light green shoots of other plants. Its oil would speed healing.

Samson broke several branches at their tip where the leaves would be the freshest and rubbed them over his wounds. Wincing, he treated all scratches.

His stomach growled. He set a few traps in an isolated pool, then collected wild figs and old berries, already dried on the brambles. A meager meal for how faint he felt, but he would not return to the carcass. Even the memory started him shaking again over the closeness of death. He leaned against a tree.

The sun warmed him, making him drowsy. The fight had left him exhausted. He slept.

The day was well spent when he woke. He ate the trapped fish and some more figs. Licking his fingers, he wished for his *ima*'s fig spread. Honey would have made it great.

He applied more comfrey to his wounds and put on his dried tunic, concealing its rips with his belt. The effort tired him, and he slept again.

When he woke the sun had welcomed a new day. He listened before moving. On the hillside facing him, he watched movement on a deer path.

Two figures came into sight. He watched their progress. Their voices carried down the slope.

If he didn't know better, he would have thought—he shook his head. Why would they come here?

But the closer they came, the more he knew.

Samson rose. *"Ima, Abba*—what are you doing here?"

His *ima* breathed deeply. Her hair was disheveled. She collapsed in his arms. "Here's your water skin."

"Looks like you've been running!" He said it in jest. He remembered how he left. Their disagreement seemed a long time ago. He felt embarrassed now at his angry outburst and departure. Slaying the lion had reminded him of how important his family was.

But why would they follow him?

He looked over his *ima's* head at his *abba*. Surely, they had not traveled these two days just to give him his water skin! He met his father's gaze, his eyebrows raised in question.

Manoah nodded. "We ran part of the way. *Ima* didn't want to miss you."

"But why did you come?"

Ima interrupted. "We consent."

Samson smiled, the disagreement forgotten. This was better than he could imagine. By his parents' consent, he felt no remorse nor hindrance to marry Tia. "Come, meet her." He shook his cloak from the leaves that stuck to it while he had rested on it.

Manoah stopped him with a hand on his arm. "We only came to tell you."

Z'llpunith added, "We must return to move the flocks before harvest."

Samson looked from one to the other. Their people always expected a Philistine raid around harvest, so they hid their flocks in secluded hills. "Of course."

He could already hear the villagers' condemnation that he had forsaken his father again.

His father's expression held no judgment.

They rested briefly, eating flatbread and dried figs his *ima* had brought. He added more fish he had caught in the still pools of the stream.

They spoke of nothing much until Samson leaned back against a tree trunk and asked, *"Abba*, what makes the angel of God, wonderful?"

Manoah's eyes widened, but he smiled. "When I asked whom we should thank for our deliverance, he responded, 'Wonderful.'" He shrugged.

Ima added, "To be delivered from bondage, fear, destruction—wouldn't that be wonderful?"

Manoah nodded. "Often we don't know we are bound until after we are delivered from it. Then we know freedom."

Samson put the last bite of flatbread in his mouth and chewed. His chest tightened as he felt the lion's claws rip his chest, again like some returning nightmare. His hair rose on his neck. A wave of fear and hopelessness shadowed him. Was this what his people felt every time the Philistines attacked? Would his fear haunt him like it did them? He shivered. He would do anything to have freedom.

Should he tell his parents about the lion, so they would be watchful? He shook his head. That deliverance was for him alone. He would keep it to himself.

Maybe fear would motivate him toward deliverance.

Before they separated, Z'llpunith hugged Samson. As she released him, she whispered, "Remember the Lord. Obedience will bring you what you desire."

A nother day of traveling brought Samson to the city before the gates closed for the day.

He retraced his steps to the courtyard wall where he found Tia; then followed the wall to the main entrance.

He hesitated, adjusting his cloak to cover his torn tunic. He felt not only the difference in culture, but in social standing. Tia's father was a man of great wealth. He pulled the drawstring to ring a bell.

A servant answered.

Samson fidgeted. "I'm here to see Tia."

The servant's eyebrows rose. His lips closed in a straight line.

Had he come to the wrong door?

Light footsteps approached the door.

Tia peeked around the servant and smiled. "The brave, wild man has returned." She motioned for him to enter and addressed the servant. "Set another place at the table."

The servant disappeared.

Samson stepped inside. The stone floor felt cool through his sandals. Elaborate tapestries hung on the walls and over windows.

He smelled again the peaches and honey. "I've come unexpected. Perhaps I should return later."

She laughed. "You're in time to meet my father."

She led the way through an open, bright corridor to another room.

He had only eaten fish and figs for several days. Smells of roasted meat, sweet pastries and fruit met him. His mouth watered.

Tia approached a man seated at the head of the table. "Father, this is the man I told you about." She turned to Samson, "This is Gaines."

Samson had come too early for visiting. He stood awkwardly, not knowing what to do.

The man wore only a tunic, tied around his well-rounded figure. His head was uncovered. Without rising, Tia's father scrutinized him from head to foot.

Samson felt his own uncouthness. He had removed the comfrey compresses before entering the city, but their smell clung to his clothes, along with the wild smell of dirt and wildlife. His tunic was shredded, although he'd tucked what rips he could beneath his belt. His hand-woven tunic seemed coarse against the rich silks of the table coverings. His hair, long according to the Nazirite vow, was braided in seven long tails behind his back, in sharp contrast to his host's bald head.

Tia's father finally finished his study and gestured to the seat beside him. "Wild man, welcome."

Samson looked at Tia. "My name is Samson. I come from the village of Zorah."

"A Jew?" His eyebrows rose as he looked at Tia.

Tia sat beside Samson. "My father is an important ruler of this city."

Samson bowed his head. "I am honored to be permitted to eat with you."

Tia hesitantly looked at her father. "He knows Lucas."

"Lucas?" He shrugged in a surprised gesture. "Indeed, you are full of surprises." Then he motioned to the table, covered with foods. "Eat."

Samson thought of the prayer of blessing his father would say before their meal. Samson hesitated. He needed not bow his head, nor say it aloud. He could just remember to thank God for his protection, especially with the lion; His care by sending his parents as a peace offering to their argument; of His love—he looked up at Tia to see her watching him with a slight smile.

He felt his face flush and finished his prayer with his eyes open, then reached for the meat on the closest platter.

Tia's father gestured to several vessels scattered across the table. "Drink."

Samson glanced in one. It appeared clear. He poured some and tasted. He expected water. The drink had a faint taste of peaches. It coated his tongue with its flavor and soothed his throat like melted butter. Wine! He wouldn't insult his host, but as a Nazirite he must have no wine.

He thought of the dog, of the wine, of Tia who hovered beside him. What was his Law but restrictions that kept him from living? Perhaps this was the freedom God wanted him to experience by His deliverance from the lion!

He took a bite of lamb. The rosemary and chives enhanced the meat's flavor. He closed his eyes to savor each bite.

Tia delicately bit into her melon. "You like?"

He took another bite. "I've had nothing like it. The flavors burst in my mouth and fill my nose."

She laughed. "You make eating an adventure." She placed on his plate a different kind of meat. "Try this."

It was white meat covered in a spicy-smelling sauce.

Samson tasted it. He raised his eyebrows. "I've never had anything like it; what it is?"

"It's pork, slowly roasted, brushed with a baste that keeps the juices inside."

At the name of pork, Samson stopped chewing. Pork was forbidden by Law. He remembered watching the pig in the corrals outside the city. The man was not mistaken by its good flesh. Samson lowered his head and tried to finish his mouthful. What should he do?

Tia watched, her smile changing to concern. "You do not like?"

Samson shook his head and swallowed. Perhaps the Law was written for someone else. What could he do but be a polite visitor? He smiled to reassure her.

He would have loved to eat an entire plate of that pork. But now that he knew what it was, it turned his stomach sour.

The pastries were nothing like the thin crackers of matza. Their flaky crusts were glazed with honey, sprinkled with almonds, and filled with apples, pears, and figs.

He bit into one. Peach spread with cheese dripped from it. He licked his fingers and finished the pastry in another bite.

Tia leaned over and whispered, "Those are my favorite."

Samson thought of the cheese spread. The Law, again, said they should not drink milk with meat. His *ima* was strict about that law, saying anything made from milk shouldn't be eaten with meat. Samson had been hungry, but now, looking at his unfinished plate, he wondered what other laws he had disobeyed.

Instead of finishing what he had, he chose a melon slice: its flesh—delicate, juicy, and ripe. Its juice soothed his throat and his conscience. Was he delivered from the lion to be free from the Law's bondage? Was that the freedom he wanted?

A fter the meal, Tia led him to the garden where they had talked before. This time she found a shaded area away from the fountain. She sat and patted the bench beside her. "Tell me what you have done since you left."

"How do you know Lucas?" Samson tried to keep the demanding tone from his voice.

She blushed and shook her head. "It's nothing."

"It is *not* nothing. You used it to place me in better graces with your father. And your father's expression changed at his name. Who is he to you?"

She turned away, bashful to answer. "Lucas has spoken to my father for me."

"To marry?" Samson's voice broke. His emotions plummeted from anger to despair. How could the only suitable woman he had found be claimed by his best friend?

Tia nodded. She hastened to add, "My father hasn't given consent."

"Why?"

She shrugged. "I wasn't sure—He wasn't ready—Then you came and—" Tia shrugged at him, embarrassed.

Could he hope? Samson hesitated, but had to know. "You would marry me?"

Her face turned crimson. She nodded bashfully.

He laughed heartily. "It's better than I thought for I have come to ask your father, if you're willing.

"I've thought of nothing but you since we met. Your face comes to me in the night while I sleep, and I sleep better for it. Your face shines on me during the day, and I work harder because of it. I must have you for my wife. And since you are willing, what is keeping me from asking your father?"

She grabbed his hand. "Nothing."

"Will there be a problem with your father being a leader?"

Tia laughed. "The leaders will look with pleasure on another day to feast."

Her smile faded and her cheeks paled.

"What is it?"

"Who will tell Lucas?"

Samson smiled. "Leave Lucas to me."

B efore Samson returned home, Z'llpunith began planning for the wedding feast, for as the groom's family they would host the celebration on the third day of the seven days of feasting. She would make lists of food, preparation, and extra help needed. Maybe the busyness would help her to not think about the heaviness in her heart.

When Samson returned home and found her busy with plans, he

stopped her. "*Ima*, we won't be getting married here. Nor will the village come."

"But this is your home . . . what about family? Your uncles and aunts will want to celebrate—" At his look, she stopped and lowered her head. Her chin trembled. She felt pressure behind her eyes as tears filled them.

Manoah touched her arm. He lifted her chin so she could look into his face. "What is it, Z?"

She could not hold her tears back any longer. "All my married life the women of this village criticized me. I couldn't give you a child. When I had a child, I couldn't train him. When he didn't follow you in your trade, they said I had failed again. Now as Samson prepares to marry outside our village, I am howled at, like a dog, even by the children. I get my water before the sun rises or when the sun is the hottest. I do my laundry when no one else is there. Manoah, I can never please them. And now we won't feast here in our village. What will they do to me then?" Her tears were streaming down her face. She ignored them.

Manoah did not. He wiped each one with his thumb. "Z, when you had no child, the villagers did not see you beg the Lord for a child. When the angel of the Lord appeared only to you, the village women were jealous. When they bicker about your training and teaching the Nazirite vow, they resent what you've done that they did not. When they howl, they show they do not love the Lord as their God or they would know why you do what you do.

"You gave me respect when we had no child. That was worth many sons to me. You gave our child the knowledge of the Holy One. That was worth all the training anyone could have. You gave Samson freedom to do what God directed. That will bring our deliverance.

"When I see you, I see a woman who strives every day to please her husband, care for her children, and know her God. That is all you must do. And that is enough. God is well pleased."

Samson clapped as Manoah finished. "Well said, *Abba*. I, for one, do not hold the village standard in high regard. They live in fear rather than trust. And they blame you for what they *think* I should be doing but know nothing of what God has done in the past for our people.

"You, both of you, follow your words with devotion that warrants my respect and admiration."

He hugged his *ima* and *abba*. "I'm sorry, *Ima*, you cannot work yourself to death to prepare our wedding feasts. I'm sorry you won't be so tired you will not enjoy the feast given at her house. I'm sorry you will merely come to eat and not have a bit of work to prepare, but that is what is expected of the groom's *ima*."

Z'llpunith laughed at his remarks. "When you put it that way, maybe I can enjoy the wedding feast."

M anoah went with Samson to meet with Tia's father for the wedding dowry and arrangements. Their customs were different. Their expectations unique. Manoah asked many questions and tried to honor the Lord, but he had to remind himself of his own words to Z'llpunith. They had taught Samson the Law. They could not make him obey it. Nor could he make a Philistine follow the Law when they did not know the Law Giver.

Manoah returned without Samson. He hugged Z'llpunith. "The plans are made."

"Are they much different than what we do?"

Manoah hesitated. How much should he tell? "With our people, families are united in marriage. The groom is held accountable to protect the woman. The Law makes sure she is provided for."

Z'llpunith prompted, "But their way?"

Manoah stepped away from Z'llpunith. "No one protects the woman. If she's not cherished, everyone suffers."

Z'llpunith nodded. "It seems a strange way to start a new life together. No payment for the woman is given?"

Manoah shook his head. "Unless they deceive us as foreigners. Even Samson seemed surprised he would not provide a promise of his care and faithfulness."

"Don't they stay married?"

Manoah shrugged. "Their family structure seems frail. Beggars fill the streets, uncared for by their own families."

"Samson spoke of wealth and prosperity. Remember the silks and produce?"

Manoah nodded. "Depends where you look. Behind the layers of wealth there's a deeper yearning for purpose—a sad existence."

"How was Samson?"

"His eyes are sun-glazed and love-sick. He would do anything for that woman, if she will treat him right."

Z'llpunith pressed, "Will she?"

"She cares for him."

Z'llpunith nodded. "Until?"

"You worry about something that may never happen."

Z'llpunith shook her head. "Marriage is not for differences to unite, but for two of the same faith to stand together with God."

S amson walked with his parents to Timnah for his wedding. Tad had begged to remain behind with his cousins. He was permitted. The cool morning made traveling more pleasant. By evening of the second day, they reached the stream where they found Samson the first time.

His parents had not spoken any more of his need to follow the Law.

Samson did not disobey. He merely adapted the Law to the Philistine culture to gain his wife. Wasn't that part of the freedom of the delivered?

His feet danced over the path. His heart sang. He would soon be wed, and nothing could take her from him.

How should he prepare for the differences in culture?

Tia had brushed aside his concerns by saying, "The wedding customs will fit your wildness and quest for adventure."

When he asked what she meant, she laughed but refused to say.

Now he wished he had pressed for details. Should he have brought more family? Would some of their practices transgress the Law and offend his parents? There were so many little things he had done lately that were forbidden in the Law. This new freedom weighed down on him rather than giving him peace.

They drank at the stream.

His *ima* dozed against a willow tree. She looked exhausted.

He had heard her crying the night before. Samson didn't understand such tears. He was only getting married.

His father lay on his outstretched cloak. He looked like he would rest for a long time.

While they rested, Samson hiked to where he had left the lion carcass several weeks ago.

He expected the carcass to be torn apart and the bones scattered. But as he approached, it was still intact. He slowed his steps, cautious. Coming closer, he understood.

Bees had built their hive in the lion's gaping jaws, keeping any animals from eating its meat.

Pulling his hood over his head and tucking his cloak belt in securely, he reached into the lion's mouth and scooped out a handful of honey.

The bees swarmed around his head. Their stings penetrated only partially through his sheepskin cloak. Several stung his hand.

He backed away, licking his fingers.

The honey was made from the early spring flowers. Its delicate flavor hinted of clover blossoms.

This would be the very thing to strengthen his *ima*. When he reached the stream, he found them awake.

He offered them the honey, but didn't tell them from where it came.

Had he forgotten the Law that said not to eat from, nor touch, any dead thing? "No," he told himself, "I have merely made sense of the Law." After all, honey came from an unclean insect already, and it was allowed. Why should he not eat it now?

CHAPTER 8

When they reached Timnah, Z'llpunith followed Samson and Manoah through the city streets. Z'llpunith clung to Manoah's hand as the crowds pushed them through the gate and swept them down the street. She could only see Manoah's back. The noise was deafening. She distinguished no single voice, but they all melted into loudness. The smells were like coming upon a sheep that been killed by a lion, its bowels ripped open and baked in the sun. That smell mixed with food cooking. She wrinkled her nose and pulled her hood farther over her head. How did people live in this?

She raised her eyes once to see if she could see Samson. The dark street and crowds hindered her. Did the sun ever penetrate between these crowded buildings? Before glancing down, she caught a man's eye passing them. She shivered at what his soul reflected. What depths of evil did they hold?

She tripped and fell into Manoah.

He caught her and paused.

Darkness kept her from seeing what she tripped over. Her ankle hurt, but she didn't want to be lost here. "Don't mind me. Do you still see Samson?"

Manoah answered with a reassuring squeeze of her hand.

Z'llpunith kept her head down and moved her feet as if in a nightmare—running from an unknown evil.

Only she ran toward it.

And the evil was getting stronger.

They turned down a side street. It widened to allow light at the end. With the thinning of the crowd, they slowed their pace.

She had been squeezing Manoah's hand so tightly her hand twitched. Now she relaxed her hold.

He caught her eye and smiled.

She could not smile back; she only swallowed.

Samson led them to a door.

As Z'llpunith raised her head to look around, she gasped.

The house was a mansion! She brushed her hand down her soiled, sheep-skin cloak and fixed her hood more securely over her head. She felt inadequate to stand before the door, let alone enter.

Manoah stepped closer to her and placed his hand gently on her back.

Though reassuring, Z'llpunith felt him tremble. She looked into his face.

Manoah smiled. But his forehead was wrinkled and his eyes did not shine.

Samson looked at them both and grinned, then knocked.

Z'llpunith could not share his pleasure.

When a servant answered, they followed him through the house.

Z'llpunith stared open-mouthed at the tapestries hung on the walls, the spacious hallway. She peaked inside the doorways of the many rooms and wondered how many families could live here.

When the servant brought them outside again, she looked in amazement at the fruit trees, flowers, and beauty. All this inside the city!

She heard a waterfall and licked her lips, remembering how thirsty she was from the walk.

Tia appeared and laid her hand possessively on Samson's arm. "You took your time in returning."

Samson nodded to Tia's mother and smiled. "My thoughts were with you the entire time, yet for my parents' sake, we arrived when we could."

Tia then looked at Manoah and Z'llpunith. She embraced them.

"Welcome. My father has some business that he must attend to. This is my mother."

She gestured to a woman lounging under the fig trees her silk tunic revealing much.

Manoah nodded but looked away.

Z'llpunith pulled her cloak more tightly around her body, as if she could remove her embarrassment of the woman's exposure.

Tia clapped and a servant hurried to offer them fruit and drink.

Z'llpunith watched Manoah. She had not considered how they would obey their Law here with the Philistines. To eat with foreigners implied they were friends and united in faith. But they were not sitting and actually eating a meal with them. Was she rationalizing their behavior, as she wanted to excuse Samson's?

Manoah met her look. He licked his lips and took a piece of fruit from the platter.

The fruit did look good: melon and peaches drizzled with honey and mint. She could not remember the last time she had eaten melon. Her mouth watered at the anticipated treat. Z'llpunith took a bite. She wanted to keep the mouthful in her memory. Its delicate texture. Its refreshing, soothing flavor. The slice disappeared before she realized it.

Another servant brought a tray to pour her a drink.

She looked again at Manoah.

Manoah watched Samson, who sipped from his own vessel.

Tia's mother startled Z'llpunith, "You don't find our wine good enough?"

Manoah bowed to her. "It's not a matter of good or bad; it's a matter of devotion. We've taken an oath to drink no wine."

Tia's mother laughed as Samson poured himself another vessel. "The devotion extends only to you? What about your son?"

Samson held his vessel toward her. "My devotion ends where good wine begins."

She laughed. "Then keep the good wine coming." She again directed her attention to Manoah. "Our water is not good, but . . ." She directed a servant to bring some.

A small dog ran toward Samson, yipping excitedly.

Tia laughed. "The little traitor loves him more than the hand that feeds him."

Samson swooped up the dog and cradled it in his arms.

Z'llpunith gasped. It was one thing to imagine Samson familiar with their ways and forgetting his own, but seeing him reject the Law in such blatant ways as drinking wine and holding an unclean beast!

Those few treasured bites of fruit churned in her stomach. She felt lightheaded.

Manoah stepped to her side. "You look pale. Sit down, Z." He guided her to a bench and sat beside her.

Tia's mother asked, "Would you like to rest?"

Manoah nodded.

A servant escorted Manoah and Z'llpunith to their own chamber.

After the servant left the room, Z'llpunith covered her face. "Do we belong here?"

"Drink some water." Manoah offered his vessel.

She took the vessel in both hands and sipped. "What were we thinking to come here? How can we eat with them? Should we wait at home for Samson to bring his wife?"

When Manoah did not say anything, her heart felt dread.

She could not see his expression with his head lowered. There was something he was not saying. "Tell me."

"Samson won't be returning home."

Z'llpunith choked. "We won't see him again?" Her voice trailed off.

"Our son is not lost from us forever. He will return."

Z'llpunith sat straighter. With great emotion, she said, "Return? When he returns, he will be chewed up and spit out by this people who think not of family and what is good. He will return wasted and broken. He will not be our son with his confident, care-free way. His adventurous spirit will be gone. Return? Yes, but that will not be our son."

Manoah listened. "But you will take him back."

Z'llpunith nodded miserably. "He is our son."

Manoah nodded. "Then we are finished here until he returns to us."

Z'llpunith shook her head. "How do you just sit there and know these things?"

"Can you change them?"

"No, but—"

"Then they are not yours to hold or to change. Give them to God. He will carry the load."

Z'llpunith looked around the room. The wealth of its tapestries on the walls, the comfort of its bed, the spaciousness of its room—they did not bring comfort or peace. "Yes, we will leave."

"You won't regret we didn't stay for the wedding?"

Z'llpunith tried to read his eyes. "Do you want to stay?"

"Our son has come far from our training." Manoah paused. "It's not for us to make Samson's choices. But if we stay, our own devotion to God will be jeopardized, and I cannot live with that."

Z'llpunith nodded. "Then we shall leave."

A s Samson watched his parents leave, he felt remorse. He thought of the many wedding feasts he had attended in his home village, where the entire community witnessed and celebrated the covenant between bride and groom. Their feasts united the bride's family with the groom's family. The groom promised to protect and care for his bride until death.

Here he felt cut adrift, without an anchor, like a weed seed blown from its stalk. Should freedom hold no accountability? He blinked in an attempt to reassure himself. He knew his way home.

Tia stood beside him. "Is it hard to say good-bye to the old and grab the new?"

Samson let his eyes move from the top of Tia's head to her feet. He shook his head. "The new looks a lot better."

Tia laughed, that musical song he loved.

Samson took her in his arms. "So what is next to make you mine?"

Tia squirmed out of his arms. "The leaders come to celebrate their wildness, before marriage destroys it with a feast."

"I will do what they require. But do you think you can destroy my wildness? My wildness comes at great cost. I have forsaken my parent's teachings. Do you think my wildness will stop after you are mine?" He grabbed and held her tightly.

She stopped struggling and leaned against him.

He whispered in her hair, "You are wrong. It will only have begun."

CHAPTER 9

S amson dressed with care for the feast that night. It seemed strange not to have his parents attend his own marriage feast. But he felt freer by their absence. They were like a conscience with a critical eye. Even by their silence, he sensed correction. He could celebrate better without them.

He also felt the loss of his extended family. He did not know many from the city. How hard could it be to eat and drink with strangers?

Gaines had brought material for him to choose a new wardrobe. The rich weaves and bright colors showed Gaines ruled over many. For this night, Samson selected a rich sapphire tunic that accented his dark eyes and long hair.

He brushed his hair gently to avoid causing his head to ache and twisted it into three braids. They reached below his waist. He tied them back with a band of the same sapphire material as his tunic. His long hair distinguished him from others of the city.

He examined himself in the reflection glass on the door of his chamber. He pulled his tunic straight and threw his shoulders back.

Gaines met him at the end of the passageway. He appraised him, his eyebrows raising with a half-smile. Without a word, Gaines led him through a number of passageways to enter a spacious room, arranged with one long table set for a meal.

"Wow. You do feasts right."

Gaines laughed. "This will only be the start. We'll greet your guests at the door. They're leaders of the city you will do well to please."

Gaines introduced each guest. "This is Saraat. He leads our temple worship and gives the final word in our courts."

Samson bowed to him.

Saraat scrutinized him, taking his time.

Samson felt as if he were some meat roasted on a spit.

When through, Saraat addressed Gaines, "A foreigner, Gaines?"

Samson's village, even with their faults seemed warm and welcoming compared to this man. Samson stood taller, though shorter than any of the guests. "To rule a city's worship must feel an ominous task."

Saraat acknowledged him, his eyebrows lifting. "It is my pleasure to make sure our people are pleased."

Samson creased his forehead as he puzzled over the words. "Shouldn't worship be to please God?"

Saraat appraised him again. "Pleasing the gods is secondary to men's pleasure. For when men are pleased, so are the gods."

"What happens when men's pleasure is not what the gods accept?"

Saraat frowned. "You do not understand the gods if you think we cannot please them."

Samson laughed. "My father used to tell me, if I understand God, then my God is too little."

Gaines interrupted. "Samson, here's another guest you must know." When they had moved away, he whispered, "It's best not to argue with Saraat."

Samson nodded. He only questioned to understand. Their worship seemed to depend upon man's whims. Wouldn't that change?

Almost thirty guests arrived. Servants passed among the guests, offering drinks, fruits, cheeses and meats.

Marriages in Samson's village were times to celebrate life and to encourage family. Samson whispered to Gaines after the guests arrived. "I am curious. How do you feast at a wedding with just men?"

Gaines laughed. "I see Tia has surprised you with our customs. The first night, the women and men feast separately to worship the gods better." Gaines looked around the room. "We've waited for one more guest, but he has decided not to come." He sighed but led Samson to the seat of honor beside him at the table.

Gaines cleared his throat and announced, "Let the feasting begin."

There was general laughter and frivolity as the men took their seats around the table.

The seat across from Samson remained empty.

Before Samson could ask, servants poured into the room carrying steaming platters heaped with food.

The smells alone made Samson sigh with pleasure.

Meats and vegetables, smothered in rich sauces, were set in front of each guest.

Gaines leaned over to whisper to Samson, "Tia mentioned how much you liked this meat." He pointed to a mound in front of Samson. "We included it for you especially."

It was the pork, that had gone down so sweet, but had soured in his gut. He forced a smile and grabbed a flatbread to fill. "Then I shall truly enjoy it."

He closed his eyes. At home his father would have thanked God for the meal, but should he give thanks for something he should not eat? Or should he just enjoy it from the hands of his new family as a token of the bond he was now forging?

In a new land, with new customs, shouldn't he learn new ways? He spoke a brief, silent prayer as he chewed his first bite. What harm would it do?

The meat melted in his mouth.

Gaines smiled, watching him. "You like?"

Samson nodded. "I have missed much."

"We will try to rectify that." Gaines pointed to another item on his plate. "Try that."

The piece felt springing, almost bouncy as he scooped it in his flat bread. He bit and almost lost it down his throat. The texture was difficult to chew. It sprang back after his teeth let go of it. The flavor was strong, like nothing he'd ever had before.

Gaines nudged him. He seemed pleased to have offered it to him. "Like it?"

Samson swallowed without completely chewing it. He smiled. "What is it?"

"Our people trade with those on the coast. They catch clams."

At Samson's puzzled expression, Gaines continued. "A sea creature that lives in two shells clamped shut. A special treat for us so far inland."

Samson gulped his wine. "You honor me with your food as well as your wine." He raised his vessel. How many rules of his people had kept him from experiencing life?

Wine flowed freely throughout the meal, and so did the advice about how to be wild before Samson was caged.

One man shouted from the other end of the table. "Hey, foreigner."

Samson swallowed before turning toward the voice. Would they insult him before their host?

But Gaines did not acknowledge the insult.

The speaker seemed pleased with the name. "Foreigner," he began again. "Tell us how you seek pleasure from the gods."

Samson gulped from his vessel and put his cup down.

All the eyes of the men were riveted on him, as if judging his worth by his answer.

He pushed from the table and swallowed. "Our people do not seek God to *find* pleasure. We seek God to *give* Him worship."

Another man laughed. "Worship?"

Saraat, the man beside him, interrupted. "No god can be worshipped without man's pleasure."

Samson corrected him, "Man does not dictate to God what He should accept. Man humbly acknowledges what God wants from him."

Saraat spat. "We have slaves for that. No god will tell me what I should do."

Samson tried to explain. "Our people don't eat what you eat." He pointed to the plate before him. "Our rules do not allow it."

They looked confused. "Why would your God keep you from enjoying life?"

As Samson had tried these foreign foods, he also had wondered what was the harm. "When I was small enough to sit on my father's knee, he said, 'Life has many things we don't understand. One of them is God. Since we can't understand God, we won't always understand His rules.'"

Gaines slapped him on his back. "But our gods are easy to understand, are they not men?" He looked down the table. "We use them for our own enjoyment." He pointed to the servant standing against the wall.

The servant nodded and left.

Gaines smiled. "We will bring on *our* worship of our gods."

The men laughed and settled more comfortably on their cushions.

Gaines whispered to Samson, "Don't seek to change our worship. You do not want Saraat's wrath."

Musicians entered. Those with drums entered first, arranging themselves in the corner. They beat a rhythm almost warlike in its beat.

Lyres followed. Instead of soothing notes, the melody sounded haunting, with jarring breaks that emphasized sadness.

Samson leaned back on his cushions. Instead of inciting a warmth, the music made him feel empty, hollow, like his life was being sucked from him.

He studied the men around the table. Many had blank looks, like the music had dulled their wits.

He watched Gaines out of the corner of his eye.

Gaines was no older than Samson's own father. His father worked hard, Gaines did not. Yet his father had peace and happiness, even with the hardness of his life. Gaines looked resigned with his life, as if by just living he was weary, yet all he had to hope for.

The music drew Samson back to its haunting feeling. How could music be so wrong? Didn't it reflect the heart of the people? Or was that why he felt so empty?

Samson longed for what he knew: the music, the food, his family, even the villagers. Not just because they were familiar, but because they were right.

The lyre stopped.

And with the silence that followed, that haunting, possessing feeling lifted.

Samson breathed more freely.

The drums continued to beat. The beat made him tap his foot and nod his head.

Movement from the doorway caught his attention.

A dancer entered. Her hair fell down below her waist in long dark curls that shimmered with every movement. Her silks were thin and translucent, enabling her movements to be enjoyed. She was beautiful. Her eyes found his; they shined with excitement and invitation.

Samson watched in silent appreciation.

Gaines leaned over to whisper, "You like?"

Samson could not speak. He had seen nothing like this before. He glanced at the other men. They all seemed hypnotized by her. "Is this the pleasure you spoke of for the gods?"

Gaines smiled. "You learn quickly. She's my other daughter."

With his people, a father protected his daughter until married. She would not be displayed in front of a group of men. Samson stuttered, "Your daughter?"

Gaines nodded. His proud expression made Samson turn his attention back to the dancer. What kind of people encouraged this from their daughters?

Saraat nudged Samson. "When you grow weary of your wife, it is good to know other beauties are available. Is it not?"

Samson choked on his drink. He could not imagine his own father looking for another wife. "What of the wife of your youth?"

Saraat laughed. "Of my youth? That was four women ago. When you tire of one, there're plenty who will find rest in your chamber."

One man shouted from the far end of the table, "Hey, foreigner."

Samson cringed at the slur again, but he turned and faced the caller.

"Since your God allows you no pleasure, what do you think of ours?"

Samson looked around the table. "Your gods seem more like figures with men's skin," He paused and gestured toward the dancer, "But I could learn to be pleased by them."

The men laughed.

Gaines smiled. "You will do well with us, Samson."

The door to the courtroom banged opened.

The music and talking stopped.

A man stood in the doorway, silhouetted by the torches burning behind him.

The last guest had arrived.

Lucas.

Lucas did not look directly at him, but Samson felt undone. His look challenged and threatened him.

Samson lifted his half-filled vessel toward Lucas. "To the wildness of Lucas and his pleasure."

Others lifted their own vessels, repeating the toast, and emptied their cups.

Samson stepped forward to greet his former friend, but felt stopped by an invisible wall.

An awkward silence followed.

Twenty-nine men behind Samson watched.

Lucas's stare radiated hate; he looked over Samson with disdain.

Turning from Samson, Lucas greeted Gaines. "You honor me with an invitation."

Gaines responded, "You decided to come."

Lucas shrugged. "It is for Tia I came."

Samson felt awkward standing. His arms hung loosely at his sides. How dare Lucas intentionally come late to make a grand appearance, rebuffing him in front of men who thought they were Samson's superior. He clenched his fists. They tingled as if he'd touched fire.

He retraced his steps and sat again.

Lucas followed him to the table and sat across from him. He hissed. "You are not worthy of her. You can't even supply your own wedding clothes."

Samson swallowed.

Lucas laughed.

But he had misread Samson's reaction as fear. It was not fear, but anger. Rage his *ima* had warned would someday cause great grief. He shoved that motherly advice far from his mind as he spoke. "You've come at just the right time."

He waited for the attention of all the men and raised his vessel. "I have a riddle for all of you." Samson paused. "But let us make it worth your effort. . . If you answer it correctly within seven days, I will give you thirty linen wraps and thirty changes of clothes. But." he paused for emphasis, "if you are unable to answer me, then *you* shall give *me* thirty linen wraps and thirty changes of clothes."

Gaines's face lit in a smile. "Excellent."

Saraat shouted, "Tell us the riddle."

Samson raised his hand for silence. He studied each face, memorizing them, then began: "Out of the eater came something to eat; Out of the strong came something sweet."

He paused, drank, and sat down. He looked across the table at Lucas and nodded.

The men murmured amongst themselves as they questioned what it could mean.

Samson finished his wine and nodded to Gaines. Lucas had taken any enjoyment from the feast. "The meal was flawless. The entertainment was delightful. But I find myself weary. If you might excuse me?"

Gaines looked nervously between Samson and Lucas. "It is not normal."

"Nor do you feast with a Jew every day."

Gaines leaned forward and lowered his voice. "I cannot allow you to leave until we go to the temple. Our gods must sanction your wedding."

Samson conceded.

Gaines rose and announced, "Although out-of-the-normal, we will move to the temple early at our groom's request."

Saraat chuckled. "Early arrival means longer to enjoy."

The leaders made their way through the city streets to the temple. In front of the temple, a circular courtyard extended underneath a balcony supported by ornate columns. Everything was tiled with rich stones of precise workmanship.

They did not loiter in the lower courtyard but ascended the temple stairs to another open courtyard where an altar sat in the center.

The leaders knew what was expected, for immediately they called for the entertainment and vied for a prominent place on the balcony to watch the courtyard below.

Samson stood by Gaines as the favored guest.

Servants appeared as if by unspoken request, bringing drinks.

Other servants pushed crates of—Samson whispered to Gaines, "Looks like they cleaned the streets and collected the remains."

Gaines laughed. "That's what they've done."

"What for?"

Gaines nodded toward the lower courtyard. "For him."

As he spoke, a blind man was pushed to the center of the courtyard. He wasn't blind by disease or birth. His eyes had been stabbed and left hollow.

Gaines motioned to the man. "He took Saraat's daughter without asking."

Samson nodded but did not understand. If they freely married and remarried, what harm would there be if a man took without asking? Or was it because she was Saraat's daughter?

The man was stripped of his clothes, twirled in circles, yet kept in chains. When they stopped spinning him, he staggered across the courtyard. When he almost reached the balcony, two leaders motioned for the servants to dump the refuse over the balcony. It splattered over the man.

Those watching hooted as the man slipped and fell.

More crates were emptied.

The smell rose to the balcony.

The wine and rich foods churned inside Samson. He was pressed against the railing by others and could not leave. Having nowhere else to turn, Samson leaned over the balcony to lose what he had eaten.

And hit the man on the head.

Saraat clapped him on the back. "Well done. Enjoying our amusement, eh?"

Samson hid his disgust. His act encouraged others.

They began spitting and urinating over the edge.

Samson could only step back and look away.

The leaders soon grew weary.

87

The man was hauled away.

Another was brought out. This time a woman.

She wore a mask. She was disrobed. Instead of refuse, the men hurled insults and catcalls, commanding dances and movements.

Samson leaned toward Gaines. "What did she do?"

Gaines's expression was one of bewilderment. "She was found in some farmer's house. What a find, eh?"

Samson remembered girls from his village who had disappeared after a Philistine raid. Is this where they were taken? Samson turned his back on the spectacle. "What will happen to her after this?"

Gaines motioned to the doors that lined the courtyard. "She will stay in one of those."

Samson did not want to know, but something compelled him to ask, "Will she ever leave?"

Gaines placed his arm around Samson's shoulders. "Most of the temple's offerings only last a year at the most."

"Where do they go after that?" Samson moistened his lips. He would not drink anymore. His head already felt light. Though he had lost his dinner, he felt weak.

Saraat injected, as he motioned to the altar. "Dagon must be satisfied."

Samson nodded. "You kill her?"

Saraat smiled. "Kill seems like such a harsh word, Samson. We sacrifice her as an offering."

Samson again nodded, but he could no longer look at the courtyard below.

He counted the doors that lined the courtyard.

Thirty doors.

Did thirty young girls wait behind each one for whatever anyone wanted from them?

No wonder they covered her eyes with a mask. How could any woman endure such abuse without losing her soul?

Samson leaned toward Gaines. "I appreciate your hospitality, but I do not feel well."

Saraat leaned over his shoulder and spoke conspiratorially to

Gaines, "He can't leave without pleasing the gods. Even if he is a Jew." He spat out the final words.

Gaines lowered his voice. "You must celebrate your manhood to the gods before you can return home."

Saraat laughed. "Do not look so forlorn, foreigner. It will be to your liking."

Samson did not want to say that nothing of their entertainment had been to his liking. The women had, if he could forget his values of what was good.

Gaines nodded to the doors. "Pick a door and enter."

Samson swallowed. Wouldn't he betray Tia?

Saraat nudged him. "Pick a door. Once you enter, nothing will be the same."

Samson swallowed and entered the first door.

The room was dark with a single candle glowing on a small stand. Incense burned giving him a heady feeling. A young girl lay on a bed. That was all the room held.

Even in the dim light, he saw fear in her eyes. He could not do this, even if it meant not marrying Tia. He turned to leave.

He groped for the doorknob.

There was none.

He turned to the girl. "How do you get out?"

Her voice was without life. "Once in, there *is* no leaving."

"How do *I* leave?"

She sat and leaned forward. "You don't want to hurt me?"

"No, why would I hurt you?"

She shivered. "Because that's what men do. But the women are worse."

Samson coughed. "Women come here too?"

She nodded.

He did not want to know anymore. He pounded on the door.

"Stop!"

He stopped but did not turn around.

"You pull that string when you want out." She pointed to a string attached to the ceiling. "But, wait."

Samson had stepped toward the rope, but he stopped at her request.

"If you stay longer, I won't be hurt by another."

Samson shook his head. "More will come tonight?"

The girl nodded. "They come all night, then during the day."

Samson looked at the string. "When the door opens, why do you stay?"

She laughed but it held a mocking note. "I am tied."

Samson looked closer.

Her feet and hands were tied.

"But how—?" he could not voice his thoughts. He wiped his forehead. The incense was making him unable to think. If he stayed much longer, he would do something he would regret.

He pulled the string.

Within moments, a servant opened the door from the outside and let him out.

He breathed the fresh air deeply.

Lucas stood outside his door.

Lucas's eyes registered surprise. "Finished so soon? Not much of a man."

Samson glanced at the other doors. He glimpsed Gaines entering one and Saraat's back as he shut another door. All the other leaders were disappearing behind doors. There were only thirty doors. Lucas had been the thirty-first. "Had to wait?"

Lucas shrugged. "Knew you'd finish first."

Samson thought of the girl inside. "This is no test of manhood when a man attacks a tied, helpless girl."

Lucas laughed. "Depends on how many you can do in one night. You couldn't even take one."

Samson's brow wrinkled. He could not find words to banter back.

Lucas laughed as he slipped into the room.

Samson stumbled down the temple stairs and ran back to Gaines's home. He had seen enough of pleasing the gods to know his God was good, even with all His rules.

CHAPTER 10

The banquet was in its second day. The men congregated at Gaines's house before Samson arrived.

One leader complained, "I can't afford to purchase my own clothes, let alone give this foreigner thirty complete changes of clothes."

"What did you want us to do—let him think he could best us?"

Saraat turned to Gaines. "Why did you invite this foreigner? Did you want to ruin us?"

"What kind of wealth does this man have that he could promise thirty full changes of garments."

"He thinks he'll win."

"What arrogance!"

One voice rose above the others. "Can anyone answer the riddle?"

The disputing stopped. All looked at the others.

"Come on, men, it can't be that hard." Lucas leaned forward and spoke in scheming whisper, "We can't solve the riddle."

Another interrupted, despair coating his words. "Then we are undone."

"But," Lucas paused until he had their attention again, "we know someone who can."

"Who?" several shouted.

Lucas raised his hand to quiet them and scowled. "Tia will tell me."

"You are deceitful, Lucas. But we like it."

Lucas smiled for the first time.

L ucas felt the eyes of all the men as he left the banquet hall. His footsteps sounded loud along the quiet corridor.

He had always kept to himself, not joining in the activities of others. That's what attracted him to Samson the first time.

They had both been misfits, wanting to change what was wrong, but not knowing how. Both resented rules. Their long discussions brought no solutions, except to build a bond that was hard to break. Until now—

Samson had crossed the line from friendship to traitor when he had claimed Tia. The last time Lucas had talked with Tia, they had spoken of marriage. When Lucas received the wedding invitation for Samson and Tia, without any explanation, he felt like his heart had been thrown to the dogs. He smirked. How ironic—he had met Samson over his dog's death. Whose death could come from this?

Rumor claimed Lucas wasn't willing to give up his loner ways. Pshaw. He'd already given up those by telling Tia his heart.

But tonight, no heart would be involved. By accepting Samson and rejecting him, Tia had seared a hole where once his heart had lived. There was no going back.

When he reached the ladies' banquet room, Lucas stopped a servant loaded with pastries passing through the door. "Tell Tia I have something of hers."

The servant's eyes widened, but with a tip of her head, she disappeared into the banquet room.

When the door opened a crack, light from the room flooded the hallway. Tia's silhouette framed the door's opening.

As she started to step back into the banquet room, Lucas grabbed her wrist. "Wait!"

Tia let the door shut behind her. "Lucas. You have something of mine?" She trembled slightly but held her composure.

Lucas spoke in her ear. "Samson challenged us to riddle contest If we don't solve his riddle, we'll be poor."

Tia shook her head. Her voice trembled, "What's that to me? You should be careful what you promise."

Lucas squeezed her face and kissed her harshly. "What did you promise me?"

She flinched. "What's wrong with you, Lucas? You were never so harsh with me."

"Wrong?" He grunted. "Harshness comes when a person's heartless."

"What did you want me to do, Lucas?" She stepped away from him and crossed her arms. "Wait until you finally grew up?"

"Why grow up, when the woman you trust betrays you?"

"Lucas, you told me yourself you needed time. I couldn't wait." She touched his arm.

He grabbed her wrist and brought her against his body. "What happens when he grows tired of you and goes back to his own people? Who will take care of you then? You've forsaken your own people. They won't help. But you have one chance to prove you are still one of us."

She stopped squirming and lay still against his chest. Her face was against his. "I'm listening."

"Find out from Samson the meaning of the riddle."

Tia took a pleading tone, "Lucas, Samson hasn't told me any riddle."

Lucas crushed her against him.

She squealed in pain, "You're hurting me."

Lucas whispered in her ear. "Find the meaning or more will suffer."

The men had again gone to the temple. Samson was sickened by their abuse and cruelty under the guise of pleasing the gods. He had again entered the closed door and left quickly without proving his manhood.

He was weary of feasting. And weary of the people. He wanted the wedding to be over. And this was only the second night.

Samson lay beside Tia in their bedchamber. His newly made tunic lay over a chair for the next day when he would dress for another feast.

Tia snuggled closer to him. "How did you like the feast?"

Samson shrugged. "I grow weary of them."

Tia's eyebrows raised. "Did you like the clams and pork?"

Samson nodded, but his thoughts were elsewhere.

Tia stroked a strand of his hair away from his face. "What is it, Samson?"

Samson lay back against his outstretched arms and looked at the ceiling. "The people care nothing for you or me. They come for your wine, food, and entertainment."

"How are your people different?"

Samson hesitated. It was hard to describe commitment when a culture did not have it. "When a couple marries, they marry into a community."

"What does that mean?"

Samson thought for several moments. "I think it's the Law that brings our people together. We have safety."

Tia burst out laughing. "Safety!" She leaned away from him. "I thought you wanted to get as far from your people's laws as you could. Isn't that how you found me?"

Samson pierced his lips and closed his eyes. "The Law makes everyone accountable for himself to his neighbor. When someone disobeys, the community is responsible to remind him of the Law. I hate rules, but what I hate more is the people who corrected my *ima* for nothing she had done wrong. Their superior attitude made me angry."

"We don't follow rules. Isn't that what you wanted?"

Samson licked his lips. "Your people do what they want, when they want."

"Isn't that good? No rules restrict them."

"It isolates you."

"But you are here with friends."

Samson contradicted her, "Your father's friends. But not really his, either. He must act a certain way to remain in his position. That is a precarious position.

"By having no standard, you have no responsibility or accountability. Expectations change with the whims of the leader. When he does not need your father anymore or like what he does, he will be gone. He has no friends. These people deceive and hide behind their pleasures."

Tia sighed. "You make pursuing what we want a bad thing."

Samson shrugged, then smiled and watched her. "I enjoyed your sister's dancing."

Tia's eyes flashed in anger.

He laughed at her reaction. "But she is only half as beautiful as you."

Tia smiled. She started to say more but stopped. She grew somber. "Anything special happen at your feast?"

"No."

She pressed, "You men can't get together without competing. You didn't have any wagers?"

Samson thought of the competition at the temple; it turned his stomach. He frowned and shook his head.

"Nothing at the feast that was interesting?"

He shrugged, then remembered. "I gave a riddle."

Tia sighed. "You used to tell me everything. Why must I pull your thoughts from you like tearing a bone from my dog? Are you already growing weary of me?"

He turned from looking at the ceiling and grabbed her. He whispered in her ear. "Tired of *you*? Never."

"Then what's the riddle?"

He loosened his hold on her to look into her face. "Just a thing that happened when I was coming to town."

She seemed eager. "Tell me."

Samson laughed. "It's as if you have a chance to win the wager."

"What's the wager?"

"If no one guesses, I'll receive thirty wraps and thirty changes of clothes; but if they guess, I'll give the same to them."

Tia gasped. "But the men would be destitute if you demanded payment!"

"Tia," He spoke slowly, almost condescending. "And what about me, if they guess?" He flipped off his sandals and flung them across the floor. "Lucas thinks he can control what I have. He's got to think again."

"Lucas? What about Lucas?" Her voice rose in a panic.

Samson studied her. Why was she so nervous? Did she still want Lucas. But her reaction was more of fear. "Lucas is jealous," Samson guessed, taking her into his arms and kissing her. "Let's not speak of Lucas in our bed. Nor riddles. Nor feasts. Let's just enjoy each other."

T he next morning, Samson grumbled about a headache.
     Tia rubbed his back and head to relieve it.

"Don't mess up my hair!"

She lifted her hands from his hair. "Don't be obstinate, Samson. I'm only helping you with your headache."

"You'll tangle my hair so badly that I'll never get it out."

"Why don't you cut it? Wouldn't it be easier if it were shorter? I'll cut it for you."

His voice took on a harshness never used on Tia. "You'll do no such thing!"

She backed from the bed. "Sorry, I was only trying to help. The weight of your hair pulls on your head. It might relieve your headache. I meant no harm."

Samson just grunted. "Why don't you brush it, rather than yank on it. That may make my headache better."

Tia brushed his hair.

His breathing was almost deep and restful. His eyes closed.

"Samson." She whispered close to his ear. "Tell me the riddle."

Samson laughed. "I have not even told my parents, so why should I tell you?"

"But I'm your wife. Shouldn't you tell me everything?"

Samson snorted and rolled over. "No."

T ia was sipping wine at the snack table. The feasting continued
     throughout each day. They were on their third day. Men and

women now met together. The drums seemed to beat in the background constantly, making her entire head throb with its beat. But her thoughts weren't on the music, nor on her drink. Her guests danced, but she only stared ahead.

A whisper behind her startled her. "Have the answer yet?"

She looked across the room where Samson watched. Without moving her head, she spoke as her lips were hidden by her vessel. "I don't."

Lucas hissed. "Entice him as you did me, when you said you loved me."

Tia's hand shook as she sipped again. She closed her eyes so she wouldn't look back at Samson.

She felt when Lucas left.

S amson returned to their room to rest. By dusk, they would prepare for the third night of feasting.

Tia dressed in a gown that showed her beauty. She handed a necklace to Samson. "Can you help me, Samson?"

He stood behind her.

She could feel his heavy breathing as he tried to clasp the small pieces.

"This is harder than threading a needle!"

Tia laughed. "When have you ever sewed?"

Samson finally joined the clasp. He took her in his arms. "I will have you know I often threaded the needle for my *ima*. I could see better."

Tia leaned against him. She smoothed his hair from his face. "Still have your headache?"

Samson closed his eyes.

"What is it, Samson?"

Samson opened his eyes and watched her. "What did Lucas say to you?"

She could feel the heat rush to her face. Her fingers trembled. "It wasn't important."

Samson studied. "You trembled when he spoke to you. What did he say?"

"Really?" She laughed, nervous and high-pitched; not her usual musical laugh, but nervous and high pitched. She leaned against Samson, her lips brushing against his. "I'd rather blush in your arms than speak of another."

Samson laughed. "And you wonder if my wildness is gone."

Her hand wove through his hair. "So my wild husband, tell me your riddle."

"If I am to keep my wildness, I must keep my secret."

The sixth day of feasting had come. The men gathered in the hall around Lucas.

Saraat demanded, "Have you found the answer?"

Another added, "Our time is running out."

"You've only one more day to solve the riddle."

"You will pay if we cannot."

Lucas had no answer. He had pondered the foolish saying until his head hurt. Didn't they also agree to the wager? Why did they threaten him?

Before he spoke, he saw Samson and Tia enter. "Quiet. Fools! Don't give him the pleasure of seeing how much it disturbs you."

He stalked from the group, but not before seeing the laughter in Samson's eye.

Samson approached Lucas. "Notice my new wedding tunic, Lucas? It won't compare to the new wardrobe I will have tomorrow." He laughed and strutted away.

Tia turned from him, her expression one of despair.

Lucas watched for a way to approach Tia without Samson by her side. No opportunity came. As the afternoon wore on, a plan formed. He slipped from the banquet room and made his way to the kitchen.

Servants bustled back and forth with dishes and wines.

Lucas stopped a servant on his way out. "I have a message for you to deliver. I will pay silver."

The man's eyes lit up.

Lucas whispered in his ear and slipped the silver piece into his hand, folding his fingers shut around it.

The servant twirled the piece around once, then hurried from the room.

Lucas smiled. He nodded to the head supervisor and returned to the banquet room. He felt better already. He grabbed a vessel from a tray as a servant walked past him. He would have the answer soon.

Lucas watched the dancers, tapping his foot to the music. He waited, fingering his vessel, but not drinking. He would have only a few moments. But those moments would be enough.

A servant slipped into the hall and headed toward Samson.

Lucas followed, but not as quickly.

The servant spoke to Samson.

Samson hurried from the room.

Lucas took Samson's place by Tia's side. "Any answer?"

Tia shook her head. "Lucas, he won't tell."

"You have not tried hard enough."

"If enticing him won't give me the answer, what will?"

Lucas shrugged. "If you don't find the answer, we'll burn you and your father's house."

Tia's face became pale. "Lucas, you can't hate me enough to . . ." Her voice petered out when she looked into his face—she stepped from him, fear in her eyes.

Lucas stepped into the shadows just as Samson returned.

As Lucas walked away, he heard Samson say, "Some stupid fool thought my *abba* had returned. Why would he return to these deceivers?"

T he feast continued for hours. Tia tried flirting with others to make Samson jealous, begging Samson, enticing him—everything she could think to have him tell the riddle. They returned to their room after the feasting. Tia's chin trembled and her eyes filled with tears.

"What's wrong?"

She shook her head and covered her face with her hands. "Oh

Samson. Why won't you tell me the riddle? If it is such a little thing, why would it hurt?"

Samson held her. "Why the tears over such a foolish riddle?"

"It's not the riddle, Samson. You don't trust me enough to share with me. How can I help you, if you don't share everything with me?"

Samson laughed. "What makes you think I need your help?"

"I want to help you, like you told me your mother helped your father."

His face softened and he hugged her. "It's not worth all these tears, Tia."

She leaned against him. Sniffling. "But if it isn't, tell me."

Samson sighed. "Out of the eater came something to eat, and out of the strong came something sweet."

She looked into his face and blinked. "But what does it mean?"

"A lion attacked me when I came to see you."

"Oh, Samson, what did you do?"

"I killed it."

"Was that when I noticed the scratches on your hand and chest?"

He nodded.

"What happened?"

"When I returned, the carcass was still there. No animal had touched it. "

"Why not?"

"Bees built their hive inside it. Their honey was the sweetest I'd ever tasted."

Tia relaxed against him. Her voice was soft. "So, out of the eater—that would be the lion—came something to eat—that would be the honey. Yes, out of the strong came something sweet. Oh Samson, you *are* brave and wild. To kill a lion then return to it."

Through her tears and nagging, she had saved her people. She kept her head against his chest and smiled. Relief poured through her.

T he heat of the day had passed. The guests would soon start arriving for the final evening of eating and drinking. After telling Tia the answer, Samson regretted it. No secret was sure unless no one else knew it. He had stayed by her side throughout the morning meal. Even this afternoon, though he was tired, he had stayed awake to keep her from leaving. He did not trust her. Especially with Lucas hovering like a crow over carnage.

The sun would set in a few short hours, and he would be rich.

He hummed as he dressed in his final tunic of the banquet.

Tia flittered around the room like a butterfly.

"You seem nervous tonight, my love."

She stopped and rubbed her throat. "Nervous?" Her laugh was not the musical one he had loved. It was forced.

"Do not fear, my pet. I'll stand by your side and hinder anyone from bothering you tonight."

Tia's eyes darted to his. There was a desperation in her voice, "Oh, Samson, you don't need to protect me. No one would bother me in a crowd of people in my father's house."

Samson smiled, but his voice held an edge to it. "Just the same, stay by my side."

Tia's face blanched, but she nodded.

They left the room together and entered the banquet hall.

Guests had already gathered.

Wine was already served.

The sun lay close to the horizon,

Samson watched the proceedings with genuine pleasure. Lucas thought he would win. He had even tried deceit but had not prevailed. This foreigner had shown all of them.

Tia fidgeted by his side.

"What is it, my love? You've hardly eaten or drunk."

"Samson, I don't feel well, I must go to my chamber."

"I'll escort you there."

"No!" she almost shouted. "I'll go alone. I think I will be sick." She brushed her stomach, her hands in a fist, her face without color.

Samson felt remorse. Perhaps she really was sick. "I'll walk you back."

When she was settled in their chamber, he returned to the banquet hall alone.

Gaines called the guests to dine. They arranged themselves around the table.

Samson stood with his hands resting on the table. He looked at the group gathered.

The seat across from him where Lucas had sat all week was empty.

"The sun has set and the time has come for the answer to my riddle." He looked around the room at each face.

The men kept their heads down.

"Come, come. You've promised a wager for the riddle. Doesn't anyone have an answer?" Samson egged them farther. "Without an answer, I must demand wages."

Lucas stumbled into the room, out of breath. "What is sweeter than honey? And what is stronger than a lion?"

Samson nodded, pasting a smile on his face. "If you hadn't plowed with my heifer, you wouldn't have found out my riddle."

Lucas smirked. "But I have. And I won."

The table erupted in shouts of joy and praise for Lucas.

During the commotion, Samson hissed to Lucas. "No man wins when he fights me." And, without eating, Samson stalked from the room and out of the city.

CHAPTER 11

Although Samson had left the feast, he could not outrun his thoughts. How could he have trusted a woman? What a fool he'd been to think anyone would care for his heart? And what a traitor Lucas was!

Striding out of the city, he headed west. He wasn't returning home, nor back to the city until he had acquired thirty linen wraps and changes of clothes. His anger gave speed to his feet and the distance flew. The night was far gone when he paused. His anger was not spent, but his strength was.

He stopped at a grove of trees and surveyed the area for danger. He did not even have his dagger.

A small spring from the recent rains meandered through the trees. The water tasted good. The rich foods and wines could not compare to the satisfaction of water to a thirsty man.

He pulled his cloak around him and lay down. But sleep would not come. After tossing for some time, he sat up and rested his head in his hands.

If he could not trust his wife, what was left? His shoulders sagged. Isn't that why he had wanted Tia? She lived without his people's restraints.

But he had not expected living without rules to hurt so much.

. . .

T he sun filtered through the trees and shone in Samson's eyes the next morning wakening him. He rubbed his head. It ached. After seven days of wine and rich eating, it would take a while for his body to recover. He stood, stretched, and drank from the spring.

Splashing water on his face helped waken him fully. He chewed a mint leaf growing near the water. It took away the sleep and refreshed him. Without seeing anything more to eat, he drank again, then set off at a good pace.

After running most of the morning, he came to a small town. He paused, then circled the town, surveying its situation.

A river flowed on the other side.

Approaching a farmer in a field, he thumbed back toward the town's walls, "What city is that?"

The farmer paused in hoeing around his grape vines. "Ramuh."

"Where does that river end?"

The farmer leaned on his hoe and wiped the sweat from his forehead. "That's the River Belus."

He wiped his hands down his tunic. "I'm ready for a meal. Looks like you could use one too."

Samson wiped sweat from his forehead. "That I could." He followed the farmer to his house, walking through a flock of chickens picking at scraps scattered outside the door.

Before the door, they both washed their faces and hands from a basin.

Samson waited at the doorway until his eyes adjusted to the smoky, dark interior.

A portly woman bustled around, bringing flatbread, eggs and cheese to the table.

The woman spoke questions as a statement. "You've come far."

"Yes." Samson filled his mouth with a bite and chewed. "This is good."

The woman blushed and laughed like a young maiden. "Only because you're hungry."

Samson shook his head. "I haven't had a meal like this since . . ." he paused. It seemed so long ago. "Since I've been home."

The woman laid another flatbread close to his place. "Sounds like you need to go back soon."

"Where'd you say you were headed?" said the farmer.

"I didn't." Samson took another bite and glanced around for a vessel.

The woman noticed and quickly rose and brought the dipper to the table.

Samson took it and thanked her with a nod. "This water from the river?"

The farmer leaned on his arm. "Yes."

"Runs swiftly?"

"Yes."

"Do you have a vessel I could borrow to travel her?"

Both the farmer and his wife laughed, but the woman was the first to speak. "No one around here owns something that rich."

Samson shifted, feeling the silk of his tunic and the tightly woven rich material of his cloak. This city wouldn't have what he needed. "How much farther until the next big city?"

The farmer studied Samson carefully. "Are you running from something, son?"

Samson laughed. "Not running from, running to. No one's chasing me," he looked at the woman and winked. "if that's what you mean."

She blushed and laughed. Her laughter was like a grunt, but Samson liked it. It was sincere and true. But then he had liked Tia's musical laughter and look where it had gotten him.

"Well, now," the farmer balanced the chair back on two legs. "In that case, the nearest city is Ashkelon."

"No, husband. It's Ono." The woman interjected.

The farmer frowned. "Yes, but no one goes to Ono for anything. Your city to go to is Ashkelon. It sits on the coast, and you can find whatever you need there." He nodded as if answering his own problem.

Samson finished his second flatbread and sipped from the dipper. He wiped his mouth with the back of his hand and smiled. He looked around the single room. He hesitated a moment, but then asked, "Would you have a dagger or knife—for protection?"

The farmer dropped his chair on the dirt floor and limped to the corner of the room. He reached under his straw mattress to pull out a dagger. He handed it to Samson with pride. "This has protected us from many raiders who'd take our food."

Samson reached out to take it, but then dropped his hand. "I couldn't take your only means of protection. What would you do if they came again?"

The woman laughed. "You don't think we depend on just that, do you? I have knives hidden all over this house."

Samson smiled as he took the dagger. "I believe that." He removed the dagger from its sheath and balanced it in his right hand. "This is good." He untied his belt and slipped the sheath on it, positioning it on his right hip where it was accessible.

The farmer, pleased with his evaluation, smiled through his missing teeth. "The minute I saw you, I knew you knew how to use that. Not in the ways of those raiders who destroy for pleasure. You had a wildness about you that would bring destruction, but not to those who are good."

Samson studied the man more closely. This couple reminded him of his parents. They made him want to return home. He sighed. First, he must fulfill his wager.

He extended his hand.

The farmer took it and pulled him toward him in an embrace.

The woman bustled around the fire, throwing flatbread and cheese into a linen cloth. She brought the four corners together and tied it securely. "You will need food. It is far."

"How far?" Samson looked out the door to see how much time had passed as they had talked.

The sun was overhead.

The farmer shrugged. "Maybe two days, if you run. Walking, maybe four."

Samson nodded. He took the food bag from the woman and hugged her.

"You remind me of my son. He was a good boy." She patted him on the back. "I hope you find what you're looking for."

Samson hesitated.

The farmer patted him on the back. "What else do you need, son? Speak up."

Samson pulled at his cloak. The silk material would easily snag and soil on twigs and dirt. The bright color could be seen from afar. "Would you have a more suitable cloak for travel?"

The farmer cackled. His eyes twinkled. "You don't want to be struttin' down the road for all to see?" From a peg behind the door, he removed his own cloak. The muted colors and thick weave would bring warmth on cold nights.

"But I won't take yours—"

The woman smiled. "He will love to strut himself around in your cloak, if you're willing to leave it behind."

Samson handed him his cloak.

The woman laughed again. "That's all he'd wear it for, 'cause I won't allow him to wear it in the fields, that's for sure."

The woman shook the old cloak. Oxen hair and pieces of wheat stalks fell from it. "It'll suit you just fine for sleeping in."

Samson swung it around his shoulders and tied the pull strings. It reached to his feet and it smelled pleasantly of oxen and dirt. "This will do." He pointed to his discarded cloak. "Try it on. Let me see you in it before I go."

The farmer became bashful and timid. "Well, I don't know. . ."

His wife urged him, "Don't waste his time, husband. Put it on. Let me see you strut your feathers."

The man stroked the silk several times before he threw it over his shoulders. "Don't know if I've ever felt such nice things."

Samson adjusted the collar and smiled. "You look like you belong in it!"

The man glowed with pride.

"Wooooeee!" the woman praised. "Where should I stand when you wear it, ten steps behind you?"

The farmer hugged his wife. "You will stand beside me where you belong."

Samson wished he could stay longer, but he glanced at the sun through the door again. Giving them both a final embrace, he added, "I'll return when I can."

The woman called after him, "The flatbread will be waiting for you."

Samson rested during the hot parts of the days and traveled during the cool mornings and evenings. He followed the river, withdrawing when he heard other travelers. Both sides of the river offered concealment in the undergrowth. The closer he came to the coast, the cooler the weather became. He could run longer without tiring and feel rested when he slept.

The effects of the wine and rich foods had since passed. An ache still gnawed in his head, but it did not throb. He had grown used to its presence.

The flatbread, too, had been eaten before he reached the city. But he found wild fig trees, nuts, and berries that supplemented what he caught in the river and trapped in the underbrush.

He found a crab-like animal that hid under rocks in slower moving eddies of the river. It used its long, curled tail to back away from the stick Samson used. As Samson kept poking, it grabbed his stick with its claw-like pinchers and hung on, even when Samson lifted his stick out of the water.

He roasted it on a stick and pulled the shell away leaving ripples of flesh that was delicate and tender. He licked his fingers after he had finished the last one and sighed.

Wrapping in the cloak for a few hours, he slept.

He had forgotten his enjoyment for quiet in the city. Now he wondered what had drawn him to the city in the first place.

Was it his yearning to belong somewhere? His own did not receive him, but nor did the Philistines. Tia had, until—

Part of him wanted to return to Tia. She had fulfilled his heart's longing; she had awakened a need he hadn't known he had. He had loved her—he loved her still. But the hurt of her betrayal was too raw.

He remembered the look of fear in her eyes. What had she been afraid of? Could he have helped her?

He stretched and drank from the stream; then broke off some mint leaves and chewed them. The flavor reminded him of the tea his *ima* always made.

He shook his head. He must focus on what was before him. How would he get thirty sets of clothes? He spit out the mint leaves and chewed the inside of his mouth.

The sun had moved swiftly across the sky. Clouds hovered low. Would it rain? Where he lived, rain came in seasons. He wished he had asked the farmer more about this city.

He must get to Ashkelon. Perhaps then he would know what to do. He rubbed his stomach. Its churning was not just from hunger, nor from thoughts of Tia; it was over what he would do next. He had no plan. Just get to the city.

He set off again at a run. He would know what to do when he got there.

The closer to Ashkelon he came, the more travelers he saw. He withdrew deeper into the dense foliage.

When the river veered to the north, he left the forest and studied the terrain. The city's walls rose in the southwest and called him onward.

He entered the city gates just before dark.

Then the Spirit of the Lord came upon him mightily.

CHAPTER 12

S amson entered the city of Ashkelon just as the sun was setting. The gates banged behind him as he stood in the city street. The streets held only farmers and laborers hurrying to their homes within the city walls after working their fields during the day. The merchants had already closed their stalls and removed their produce.

He felt pressed and squeezed after the openness of the forest. He opened and shut his fists, relaxing them as he prepared for what he must do.

His anger rekindled as he remembered the deceit of his former friend and his wife's betrayal.

He breathed deeply. A breeze wiped the sweat from his forehead and cooled him. He licked his lips. His throat was dry. He listened as he did in the forest. There, quietness indicated danger was close. Here, danger could be heard. A door slamming down the street and a yell from an open window.

He felt that danger was near, and the hair rose on his neck. His heart thrilled with the challenge, yet his mind hesitated over the unknown. He bounced on his toes.

When he killed the lion, he had felt like this. He looked up. The sky had not darkened enough for the stars to be seen. The fading blue was lightened by the reds and oranges of the sunset.

The sky seemed to speak a message, and he felt the strength of the Lord pouring over him.

It was a feeling of power, confidence, and victory. He could not fail. Nor would he be afraid. He smiled.

He strode through the streets until he reached an area of the city with wider streets and courtyards. He jumped up to sit on one wall and looked toward the west.

The sun was setting over a shimmering water that went on for as far as he could see. He sat and stared. Nothing could have prepared him for its beauty. The sunset's reds and oranges reflected off the water. The night's darkness hovered over the water as if kissing it good-night.

The water broke in waves toward the land as if compelled by a strong force it must obey. The harbor was filled with ships, but even their size looked muted by the sea's vastness. The waters kept going, like a wheat field with no end.

The breeze was damp, not hot like their winds at home that dried the wheat heads and baked cracks in the ground. This tasted of salt. He licked his lips and turned reluctantly back toward the courtyard.

Two men were conversing.

Samson leaped down from the wall, unsheathed his dagger, and strode forward. The foliage of the fruit trees and bushes concealed his progress until he was behind one man. He stabbed him in the back, slicing upward. He removed his knife and thrust it into the other man before he realized what had happened. He wiped his blade on the grass.

Samson stripped the men of their outfits and counted two.

He piled the garments into one cloak, tied them in a knot for carrying, then jumped to the top of the courtyard wall. He glanced once more at the darkening horizon. What beauty! The red colors had deepened, reflecting over the rippling waters like blood.

He would see more blood that night, but not his own.

He moved to another courtyard and scaled the wall, finding footholds in cracks in the wall. When he reached the top, he glanced over the dark garden. There was a lone man sitting on a bench facing a fountain. He seemed in deep thought.

Samson approached him without a sound, until he was almost upon him. His foot stubbed over a raised cobblestone in the pavement, and he fell forward, stabbing the man on his downward fall.

The man didn't fall, but slouched, forward.

Samson stripped him of his garments. And counted three.

Again, he wrapped the garments in one cloak. He climbed a tree to reach the wall and jumped from its height on the other side, landing with a grunt.

The night would soon be late. Where would he find men with rich garments at this hour?

Music drifted from another courtyard ablaze with candles.

Tucking his cache in a dark doorway, he scaled the wall. Pockets of darkness concealed his movements. He adjusted his sheath, pulling out his dagger as he did. He approached a man who paced, mumbling, "You're more special to me than . . . You're more beautiful than . . ."

Samson squeezed his elbow around the man's neck and stabbed him through the heart. He whispered in his ear, "I will spare you the pain of a woman's deceit."

He dragged his body behind the trees and stripped him, placing the tied garments close to his escape route. And counted four.

He again surveyed the lit courtyard. He would not risk a battle against many. He was only one, after all. But he felt strong. The tingling in his arms had subsided to a controlled pulse.

This courtyard was not the one with music. He dropped his wardrobe over the wall. This was becoming bothersome. How should he carry all these wardrobes?

The moon hadn't risen yet, and the darkened street hid his way. His shin banged something. He traced the outline of a wheel. A cart! Why would a cart be left in the road?

Samson smiled. For his taking.

He loaded the garment bundles into the two-wheeled cart. As he lifted the handles and pushed it, the squeaking wheels seemed loud in the quiet street. Perhaps the music would drown the squeak. He headed toward it again.

His parents were told by a man of God what to do. He had only been shown a cart. But it was still the Lord directing his steps.

He should have felt tired, but he didn't. Could that also be of God?

His strength kept him moving from courtyard to courtyard.

The night wore on. The moon rose and lit the street with an eerie glow, directing his path to courtyards that held a wardrobe or two.

As he wheeled the cart toward the city gate, the sun was starting to rise.

He had thirty wardrobes, crammed in the cart.

He concealed the wagon's flashy silks and expensive cloaks with the one borrowed from the farmer. He had also acquired a servant's tunic. Hunched over the cart as he was, he'd pass for a farmer working his fields outside the gates with some of the city's slop to supplement the dirt.

He nodded to the sentry at the gate as he passed and continued east. The road was smooth, but he could not stay long on the road. He looked to the north where the rim of trees showed the river. If he skirted the forest on this side, he would veer too much off his path. How would he follow the river with this cumbersome cart?

By the time he reached the woods, he had a plan.

But he must rest first. It seemed the power had left when the need for it was no longer there. Samson wished he could summon the strength at his own will, but he would seek to be content with the power that enabled him to stay alive through his activities. Perhaps that was one of those God things that his *abba* had told him he would not understand.

A s Samson approached the field, he waved to the farmer harvesting wheat. No farmer stopped in the middle of harvesting, except for a quick meal while the sun was still shining, but Samson would not pass until he spoke to him.

The farmer took off his hat and wiped the sweat from his forehead. He muttered as he trudged to the edge of the field, "He'll expect a meal, too. . ."

When he reached the edge of the field, Samson dismounted, taking off his hat.

The farmer stopped short. "Oh, it's you, my boy." He looked over the cart and horse. "You've returned in style."

Samson tied his horse to a low tree branch. "That I have. May I take a few turns with the scythe while you rest in the shade? It's probably too early for you to break for a meal."

The farmer started to decline, but Samson held up his hand. He took the offered scythe.

The man shuffled into the shade of a tree. "Don't mind if I do. But it takes more than just swinging that thing for the wheat to fall down."

Samson laughed. "I imagine so."

The wheat fell in long, straight rows behind the scythe.

The man shouted from where he sat. "You've done that before."

"Just a bit." Samson pinched a kernel between his nails. The milky juice dripped from his fingers. He rubbed the rest of the kernels from the head and popped them into his mouth. That was pure sweetness. Like sinking his teeth into fresh-picked corn. He looked over the rows he had done.

The man persisted, "More than *a bit*. Where're you from?"

Samson rested against the scythe and wiped his face with his sleeve. "The hill country of Zorah."

The man hit his knee with his hat. "I knew it! I told my wife you were one of those."

Samson bowed his head and extended the scythe back to the man.

The farmer propped it against the tree. "I could stop for a meal. What about you?"

Samson agreed. He walked his horse to the house and tied it to a fence post near some chickens. He had stopped at the doorway to wash his face and arms when he heard the farmer.

"Didn't I tell you he was from the hill country?"

"But why was he so secretive about it? Those people are good people."

"Think, woman, he's in enemy territory. I've heard our people steal and raid from them."

"How's that any different from what they do to us!" The woman raised her voice.

Samson knocked.

Their conversation ended abruptly.

The woman bustled back to the fire, heating flatbread and stirring a pot of something that smelled good. "Tell us about your trip."

Samson told of finding the city and succeeding with his mission.

The woman looked at him. Her eyes pierced through him, almost like his mother's. "There's more to this story than you're telling. But we're glad for the news. So where do you go from here?"

The farmer interrupted. "Don't go pestering the boy. He won't come back."

"He did already."

"But he had to fetch his cloak." The farmer brought the cloak from the peg where it hung.

As Samson reached for it, he asked, "Did you wear it? It's much too hot now for it."

The farmer shrugged. "I wore it a bit."

The woman wagged her finger in his face. "He wore it to town so ev-er-y-one could see him. Did he get some looks! With his crumbling hat and this fancy cloak—"

Samson laughed. "That was one of the reasons I returned. I brought you something. Follow me."

They followed him to his cart.

The farmer saw his own ragged cloak and stroked it. "Didn't I tell you woman, he'd bring it back?"

Samson smiled. "It'll serve you better than the fancy one." He pulled his belt off and began to remove the sheath and dagger.

The man stopped him. "Won't you be needing it when you return with your wager?"

Samson looked at him sharply. "How did you know about that?"

"A group of Philistines from Timnah came, shortly after you did, asking about you. They didn't trust you'd pay your wager and wanted to make sure you did, in one way or another."

Samson bit his lip. He dug in the cart. He pulled out another sheath. This one he put on his belt. "I liked your dagger, but I found others. Do you need any other . . . items?"

The farmer's eyes gleamed and his toothless smile returned. "What've you got?"

Samson showed the knives and daggers he'd acquired.

"Didn't I tell you woman, that one dagger was enough to protect him?" He selected a bootknife from the stash and hefted it in his hand.

"The handle is small, fits your hand well." Samson commented.

The farmer smiled. "I'll take it."

The woman, meanwhile, had eyed the bundles. "You got all thirty outfits you needed?"

Samson nodded, glancing at her. "I did happen to acquire an extra one I needed a horse to pull this cart around the river."

She nodded.

Samson watched the farmer. "I thought I'd give that cloak to you."

The farmer's smile widened.

"But I also found this—" Samson dug in the cart and pulled out another cloak. He shook it out and placed it around the woman's shoulders and secured it with the strings. "For you."

Her eyes widened. Her mouth dropped open. She glowed. "I never had something this fancy. But you sure you have enough to pay your wager?"

Samson nodded as he dug along the side of the cart. He brought out a hat with a flourish and placed it on the farmer's head. "So your hat will match your cloak."

Samson sniffed. "What's that smell?"

Smoke came from inside the house.

"My flatbread!" The woman ran.

After the air cleared of the burnt bread, they ate.

The woman fussed, "Flatbread would have gone so well with the chicken."

G aines came immediately when Samson knocked at his door. He shifted uneasily. "Samson, I won't—I can't pay for you, and well, a wager is a wager."

Samson interrupted. "Send for the others. I have payment."

Gaines's eyes widened. He shut his mouth but nodded.

When the leaders were summoned, they huddled behind Lucas at the entrance of Gaines's house, eyeing Samson's cart.

Lucas spoke for the group. "We won't accept servants' wardrobes for the wager."

Samson ignored him. He made eye contact with each leader until they looked down, then tossed a tied wardrobe to each man.

As they inspected their contents, Samson heard murmurs of surprise and pleasure. Some noticed the blood stains. Their eyes widened as they looked at Samson with respect.

"Where did you get these?" One man held up a tunic trimmed in gold.

Another nudged him and showed him the stain in his own. The man shut his mouth.

Samson's scorn was evident in his tone. "Was that part of the wager? Accept the payment and be gone."

The men took their bundles and hurried away.

Samson waited to hand Lucas the last bundle. His eyes held Lucas's in an unspoken message of conquer. "I pay my debts. I keep my promises. There's no need for you to harass harmless people to make sure I do."

Lucas held the offered bundle. "How was I to know? You ran from your own wedding."

Samson's tone was firm. "Because you know me."

"Not since you stole my wife."

Samson faced him. "*My* wife said you weren't ready."

Samson removed the lines from the cart. When he raised his head again, only Lucas remained. "Was one outfit not enough for you? Do you want the one I have on?"

Lucas stepped back. "How did you get these?"

Samson's scorn dripped from his words. "You've been paid."

"Samson?" The voice was hesitant, pleading, and soft.

He knew it. His shoulders drooped as he turned toward the house.

Tia stood in the doorway. Her eyes pled for him to accept her.

Samson gulped back a response. He would not look at her. He still loved her too much. He faced Gaines and gestured to his horse. He swallowed with difficulty. "He's yours for the expenses of the feast and —" his voice was forced and hoarse as he looked again at Tia, "for your daughter."

He walked away.

Tia stumbled down the stairs toward Samson. When she reached him, she grabbed his cloak with both hands. Her eyes spilled tears. "Lucas would have burned my family. I didn't want to do it. Samson, I love you."

Samson took both her hands in his. His voice softened but grew husky as he spoke. "I was moved by your tears once. And you betrayed me. I will not be fooled again." He dropped her hands like they were fire and turned away.

Tia grabbed his shoulder. "Samson. You must believe me. They would have burned us alive."

He willed his shaky legs to walk from the courtyard.

He did not look back.

CHAPTER 13

Tad had not returned from taking the flocks to the hills. What mishap could have made him take so long? Z'llpunith glanced out the door as she ground the wheat for flatbread. She watched Manoah. With each sweep of his scythe, the wheat fell in a neat row. His age slowed him down. Yet no one in the village helped, as if in punishment that Samson had not stayed to help.

Z'llpunith shook her head. Such thoughts only made her worried and angry.

Manoah had reminded her, her job was not to change others, not even her son. He shared Moses's psalm. Something about God's time was not being like their time. A thousand years were like yesterday. She sighed. It seemed like a thousand years since they had left Samson. But it had only been two months.

To know time like God.

Or maybe it was just to look at God.

Not time.

She looked at the wheat she had ground.

It was pulverized into a powder that escaped through her sieve.

She stretched. This was getting nowhere.

She grabbed the dipper and vessel and walked to Manoah. She had almost reached him when she stumbled.

All the water spilled, and the dipper bent.

Manoah helped her stand.

Her eyes filled with tears. "I can't do anything."

"He'll come back."

She could only nod. But would he come back so changed she would not recognize him?

As if Manoah could read her thoughts, he said, "God's time. Not yours. You raised him to be a man. He must be a man without you."

Manoah turned her around. "Look! On the ridge." He pointed over her shoulder. "See him?"

Z'llpunith could smell Manoah's dirt and sweat. She could feel his excitement. But she could never see as well as Manoah. His eyes could see the hawk in the sky that she saw as a speck, or the lost sheep on the hill that she saw as a rock. "Who is it?"

Manoah's voice sounded like a boy's on a day of feasting. "Samson." Manoah shielded his eyes. "He's following that trail. We can wait for him there." Manoah took her elbow and directed her to the shade of a tree.

Z'llpunith squinted harder and saw movement. What had happened that he came home alone?

S amson's marriage had hurt but also angered Manoah. Samson had willfully disregarded his teachings. Ignoring God's Word only brought suffering. Manoah expected it. But when Samson came home, Manoah was not at peace. He was glad for his son's help during harvest, but he knew Samson was running from his problems. And that concerned Manoah.

His own heart had been stabbed when Samson shared Lucas's deception and his wife's betrayal.

But coming home was not what Samson needed. At least not to stay. He had worked. Work always puts things in focus. But farming wasn't Samson's work. Samson had other work to do. And he could not do it here.

Manoah realized now that Samson must live with the Philistines.

But how to help Samson see that?

Yesterday when they had worked, Samson cutting the wheat, and Manoah tying it in sheaves, Manoah had almost told him to leave.

Something held him back.

Was it just because he didn't want to cause Z'llpunith more heartache?

She had been like an excited mother at the celebration of her son's twelfth birthday to have Samson home again.

Manoah sighed. Separation was coming again.

After breakfast, Manoah pushed from the table. "Samson, I need your help in the barn."

There was always something to do in the barn. They had finished sheaving the wheat yesterday, but it must dry in the fields before it could be threshed. He prayed it would dry quickly, so they could hide it, before the Philistines came again.

Today, Manoah felt no hurry. It felt as if time stood still.

A heaviness weighed on his heart.

He put his hands in his pockets and looked out the barn door, over the wheat bundles. It always gave him satisfaction. A gratitude for God's blessing, in spite of the worry of a raid.

Samson put his hand on his shoulder. "*Abba.*"

Manoah's insides twisted. He sensed by Samson's tone what he would say.

Samson swallowed. "I can help today, but tomorrow—"

Manoah felt like one of those sheaves had been lifted from his shoulders. "You don't belong here anymore—"

"*Abba,* I know. I'll return to Tia and make things right."

Manoah nodded toward the hills. "Take a young goat as a peace offering."

Samson nodded. "Good idea. What should I tell *Ima?*"

Manoah tried to smile. "Don't let her tears fool you. She will know what is right. She must let her head convince her heart, that's all."

Samson laughed, "That is hard to do."

Manoah crushed Samson to himself. "We all need God's help to do that, don't we?"

. . .

T ad returned from moving the flocks with their herdsmen. Many of the pastures had not replenished from the rains and needed to be rested to grow back. He'd had to move the flocks farther from the village and deeper into the hill country for grassland. He stayed long enough to ensure their safety.

Now as he descended the hill into the fields close to his home, he felt a weight settle on him. One that he could not explain.

Samson had been home. He could tell. Without Samson's help, the wheat would not have been harvested. He bit his lip.

When he entered the house, his *ima* hugged him.

She had been crying. "You just missed Samson."

He sighed. It was always Samson. Did she even know he also had been gone?

After stuffing a piece of flatbread with meat, Tad hurried to the barn. At the barn door, he paused.

His *abba* was threshing wheat. His tunic was drenched with sweat, and he was breathing deeply.

"*Abba!* What are you doing?"

Manoah paused and leaned heavily on the barn wall. "Tad! Welcome back."

Tad finished his mouthful. "It looks like none too soon." He crammed the rest of the flatbread into his mouth and wiped it with the back of his hand. "Had to take the flocks farther south. Pasture-land was better."

Manoah nodded. He still had not caught his breath.

Tad gestured to the wheat. "You harvested it all."

"Samson helped."

Tad removed his cloak and draped it on the oxen stall. "I'll do it."

Manoah sat on a manger and watched as Tad beat the wheat. "It's a good crop."

Tad nodded.

"The flocks fine?"

Tad grunted.

"Enough water?"

Tad shrugged.

Finally Manoah took the rod from Tad. "What's bothering you?"

Tad almost shook his head, but but then he stopped. *"Abba,* God gives sons to carry on their father's work, right?"

Manoah paused before nodding.

"Then why don't you require Samson to help? You work so hard, while Samson dances to the city and feasts."

Manoah smiled. "Do you want what he has?"

Tad leaned against the barn wall. His voice reflected a yearning. "All my life I've lived in Samson's shadow. He was the special one. He was chosen by God. He could do nothing wrong. I tried to hunt, track and care for the animals like him, but I was never good enough. He always corrected me."

Tad's tone hardened, "Now he marries this Philistine. He leaves when you need him most; then he wanders home and happens to help you during harvest, when he should be here all the time. *He* should have finished this winnowing. I hate him!"

Manoah bowed his head. His voice sounded like he was talking to himself.

Tad leaned forward to listen

"I prayed, asking how I should raise Samson to deliver His people. The only answer I received was to know His Word and that would give me strength.

"When Samson was growing up, many told me I must make him follow my footsteps. And I wanted him to.

"But as I listened to God, I felt resistance to those traditions. God was going to use him in a way I couldn't imagine. In order for Him to do that, I must allow Him to train Samson differently than what I knew."

Tad interrupted, "But *Abba,* the entire village thinks you're a—" He paused unable to finish.

Manoah finished for him "A poor father." He smiled. "Do you?"

Tad paused. "You're good to me. But—"

"You think I should have done something different with Samson."

Tad could not look at his father. "Yes, but—"

"To do what everyone else does will not deliver our people."

Tad pointed to the wheat. "But what is Samson doing to help our people?"

Manoah wiped his face. He was still sweating. "When you plant the wheat, no one knows you've done your job . . . until the rains come, and the wheat sprouts and grows." He smiled. "God will bring Samson's work to completion."

Tad paced before his father. His voice raised in volume. "But the others condemn you."

"When others condemn and see only what Samson is *not* doing, they lose the blessing of the deliverance. They do not see what God *is* doing in their midst. That is a great sin. For our God demands worship, wherever we are placed.

"Comparing what God gives you, with what He gives Samson will only bring discontent. He gives you strength for what He requires of you." Manoah squeezed Tad's shoulder. "Do you enjoy farming?"

Tad threw his shoulders back. "Yes, *Abba*. I love the feel of the dirt in my fingers, of watching seeds burst through the dirt with their first leaves, the satisfaction of the harvest."

Manoah's expression softened and he smiled. "God is praised by your work. You're my son in my old age. Farming and flocks aren't a burden to you. But do not think others must do what you love. Samson couldn't, even if he tried."

Tad laughed. Samson could farm, but he could not enjoy it. "But you—"

Manoah finished for him, "I'm old and not so strong?"

Tad shrugged and smiled.

"When my strength is small, I must make sure I'm doing what God wants. Often times, when I'm weary, I'm carrying a load God never wanted me to carry. I must give it back to God."

Tad took the rod from his *abba* and tapped the wheat in frustration. "Samson makes me angry. He wears you and *Ima* out."

"We must remember to let go of what we can't control." Manoah sighed. "Look into Samson's eyes." Manoah swallowed and shook his head. "I fear for him. I see a man who knows the light of right but stands in a black hole. And he stands alone.

"It frightens me to know that is where *my son* is. I can feel the darkness creep into his heart and overtake him. He must be strong to shine the light. But his strength must come from the One Who gave him that light."

Manoah shook his head. "Not many can stand alone and be strong."

Tad studied his father. "Then why don't you make him come home?"

Manoah looked at Tad. "He is in God's Hands. I can only watch as my son stumbles to do God's will. But I do know he belongs *with* the Philistines. I don't understand it. But I know it. And that is enough to make me cry to God for His help." His voice broke and Tad stepped forward to place his hand on his father's shoulder.

Manoah shook the tears from his eyes then looked into Tad's. "I am proud of the son you've become. I couldn't do all this work anymore. It's hard to let go. But you make it easier by your devotion to the land and to me.

"But do not let the land control you, or it will consume you. There will always be another field to plow, another day to work; yet there is more to life than the land. Look to God for His strength in what He wants you to do. And it will be enough."

CHAPTER 14

When Samson planned his return, it had seemed so easy, but now standing at Gaines's door, he hesitated.

When Gaines answered, he refused to let him enter.

Samson wanted to shake Gaines, instead he punched the door. "Let me see my own wife."

The goat on Samson's shoulders bleated long in his ear. He shifted the goat from around his shoulders to the doorstep. "I've brought a peace offering for Tia."

Gaines seemed embarrassed. His voice took a patronizing tone. "Samson, I thought you hated her."

"I'm still her husband."

Gaines paused, but he would not stand aside for Samson to enter. "Because you hated her, I gave her to your companion."

Samson's heart stopped. "You gave her to Lucas?" Rage boiled up within him. He could not say anything more.

Gaines rubbed his hands together. "Isn't her younger sister— remember the one who danced for you— isn't she more beautiful than Tia? She can be yours instead."

Samson shook his head. He was already married to Tia! What did the Philistines mean when they gave their word?

He swallowed the words he wanted to spew at Gaines. How could he reason with someone who did not hold the same values?

Samson looked slowly around Gaines's courtyard to try to formulate his response. When he met Gaines's eye again, his voice was low, but it held an edge that could have sliced Gaines in half. "This time, I shall not be blameless when I do the Philistines harm."

He walked down the stairs.

Gaines stumbled after him. "Samson, don't do something foolish. That's just the way things are done. I couldn't leave her without a husband. And you had left—"

Samson left him standing there.

As Samson left, Lucas watched from the shadows of his bedchamber window. He'd heard the interchange between Gaines and Samson.

He had won.

He pulled Tia to him and kissed her possessively.

When Samson had married her, Lucas realized his loss. Initially, he had wanted to kill Samson. When Samson left, he knew Samson would return. Lucas used his time to gain Gaines's consent.

Tia had little to say in the matter. She was used property. Everyone from the city had celebrated the marriage feast. Who else would want her?

Yet Lucas would never trust her again. He would protect his heart from any woman ever finding a crack to penetrate it.

But nights were less lonely. That accounted for something.

Tia squirmed from his forced embrace. "You're hurting me."

She had become whinier than he remembered. "Do you expect me to treat you like Samson?" Lucas laughed as if it was a good joke.

Tia did not. "He never hurt me, like you do." She rubbed her wrist where he had held her from running to Samson at the door. "Your kisses aren't suggestions of love, but possessions of ownership. I don't like them."

"I wasn't like this until you forgot who you belonged to. Now I must make sure you don't forget. I have you until I tire of you. Respect me and you won't get hurt."

Tia's glare told him she knew what a lie that was.

. . .

S amson left the city, but not to run to another city in anger, like before. This time he stopped at the edge of the city's wheat fields. The wheat shimmered like moving sand. The wheat heads were full and ready to harvest.

Taking several deep breaths, he evaluated his reaction with Gaines. He'd done nothing wrong. A husband has a right to come and go when he must.

In his culture, his wife would be for life. These Philistines lacked morals! Hadn't it been she who deceived him?

A slight noise off the path startled him.

A fox carried a chicken. The last thing Samson saw was its tail as it escaped under a bush.

"Brazen aren't you. And during the day." As Samson said the words, a plan formed.

Roaming the hills as a boy, he had learned where foxes made their dens. They traveled on game trails and human paths, especially close to vineyards and fields.

They were curious.

He would use that to his favor.

They were smart.

He would be smarter.

He had never bothered them before, but now he would.

He dug several holes just off game trails inside the forest's edge. The dirt from all of the holes he moved several feet beyond each hole to form mounds.

Foxes surveyed an area before entering, often on a mound such as he made. Here Samson dug another hole.

He washed his arms to his elbows to remove his own scent.

Foxes could smell well.

The quail were raising their young.

He baited the trap with quail he snared. Their peeping would lure the foxes.

Covering the hole with dry, dead twigs that would snap when weight was on them, he finished by concealing them with leaves.

His success lay in carefulness to detail and exactness to placement.

He circled the city's pastures and surrounding vineyards and orchards making countless traps.

He would catch a lot.

S amson had rested from the day's activity and now rose when the moon was full. He could see by its light. He stretched. The distance around the city was not extensive, but he hurried.

Samson carried a bundle of pitch torches and one flaming torch. He laid them beside the closest trap. In his mouth, he held a cord. Using the light from the torch, he peered into the first hole.

Three kits peered back at him.

Samson reached to grab one kit by the tail.

They backed away from him. Their ow-wowing was threatening, yet pitiful.

The answering barks from the vixen made them yowl louder.

One charged, nipping his finger.

Its sharp teeth pierced his skin. He shook his finger and withdrew his arm.

Using a branch, he pushed them to the far corner, then caught the feisty kit. Holding it by its tail, he wrapped the cord around its tail. Dangling it by the cord, he grabbed another and tied it to the other end of the cord.

He twisted the cord around one of the pitch torches and brought the struggling pair to the edge of the wheat field. He stepped on the tail of one until the pitch sparked and caught.

The snapping and sparkling pitch was bright after the hole's darkness.

The wheat was like dry kindling.

When he lifted his foot, the two kits ran in opposite directions, the larger kit dragging the other toward him. Tying two together made them linger to ensure the field burned and they did not return to their den. Their yipping echoed in the night air.

A trail of smoke and flames followed the kits. The fire spread, sweeping across the field. It lit up the night's sky.

Samson nodded in satisfaction.

He followed his traps, finishing just before the sun rose. Clouds had formed from the smoldering fields.

He had circled part of the city, eliminating seventy-six foxes. A good job for a night's work.

He lay down behind the main path in the forest, concealed by tree boughs and slept.

He would rebait his traps and resume work the next night.

He continued throughout the week.

Samson caught three hundred foxes.

He surveyed the damage from a nearby hill and smiled.

He was no longer angry.

The sun was setting over the hills when the leaders looked over the city wall at the blackened remains of the orchards, groves and harvest. Their city would starve.

"Who did this?"

Saraat felt a sense of satisfaction. He hated Samson. He was a foreigner who thought himself better than they. He had questioned their food and judged their gods.

If Saraat could eliminate Samson, perhaps he could eliminate the doubts and whisperings of his heart that Samson's questions had caused.

He raised his voice above the others. "Samson, that foreigner, that son-in-law to Gaines."

"Why?"

Saraat lowered his voice. "Gaines gave Samson's wife to his friend."

The leaders looked over the blackened remains. They were quiet.

The time for waiting was past. Waiting gave time for doubts. Saraat had a target for his anger. He raised his voice, "Burn Gaines and his household."

The cry was repeated.

The mob took over.

As the sun sank below the horizon, a massive string of torches threaded through the city's streets, moving as a serpent moves after its prey. The crowd grew, swallowing up the streets.

Smoke drifted behind them, foretelling what was coming. They surged over the courtyard walls, surrounding Gaines's house.

Saraat led the way and pounded on the front door. "Gaines! I see you at the window."

Gaines opened the door and swallowed. "Saraat. What brings you here?"

Saraat pointed to the men behind him. "Samson destroyed our city's food. We come for vengeance."

"But Samson is not here."

Saraat smiled. "You allowed a foreigner to enter our gates as a friend. You gave a foreigner your daughter to marry as our equal."

Gaines shrugged. "What if I give both my daughters for your pleasure now?"

Saraat remembered Samson's arrogant answers to their worship. No foreigner would belittle his pleasure. He pushed Gaines aside and extended his torch toward a hanging tapestry. The flame caught and brightened the dark room with its light. "Burn them!"

Men surged forward with their torches. Some throwing them through windows, others entering and making sure their fire caught something.

Flames leaped up and caught anything that could burn, raising colors of orange, red, and yellow high in the sky.

The evening breeze took the black smoke through the city and up into the mountains.

The men had long since gone home, but still Saraat watched the flames turn to ashes.

His conscience should bother him no more.

S amson walked through the blackened remains of Gaines's house. The ambers seared his sandal bottoms and stirred puffs of smoke from the ashes.

He had watched flames leap above the city walls three nights ago from the hillside where he camped but had thought nothing of it.

But today, as he retraced his steps to Gaines's house to return the wedding wardrobe Gaines had provided, he remembered the smoke and flames.

Gaines's own people had turned on him.

Samson remembered telling Tia about Gaines not having friends. It was prophetic.

He stumbled through the ruins.

Samson felt numb, not angry. He had been angry at Tia, betrayed. But even as he had returned to claim her as his wife, he still loved her.

She had drawn out his heart. Encouraged him to share his dreams.

He had felt no pity when she had wept as she had told him of Lucas's threats to burn her father's house. Why had he not believed her?

Now he did.

They had blamed Gaines for the field fires.

Samson clenched his jaw and studied the ruins. Before, he'd had a chance to win Tia back.

Now he had truly lost her.

He felt empty.

Hollow.

Lost.

In frustration and anger, he kicked at the ashes. His toe stubbed against something hard. He picked it up.

A leather piece with studded gems had escaped the flames. He rubbed the charred leather between his fingers. Tia's dog's collar. A gem came off in his hand.

He dropped the blackened leather but placed the gem in his pocket.

Its tangible memory brought him to tears. He had lost her forever.

He knelt in the ashes and covered his head and wept. He didn't know how long he stayed on his knees, but when he stood, the sun was low in the sky.

He looked toward the setting sun. "I will take revenge; then I will quit."

CHAPTER 15

S amson rose from the forest where he had slept and untied his belt. Picking up the dagger that had lain by his head during his rest, he replaced it on his belt, adjusting it securely. He pushed down his hat and tucked his hair beneath his cloak to avoid detection. Then he entered the city. Behind him the gates slammed shut for the night.

The markets were empty now, with no produce or foods to offer.

The streets were silent.

He headed toward the wider streets that boasted larger houses of wealth and prestige.

A tapestry was pulled from the window of one house to allow a breeze. Inside, a man stood over a desk, his back to the window.

Samson drew his dagger and climbed through the window.

"You came as I expected."

"Did you expect I would allow you to murder my wife without revenge?"

Saraat turned around. His disdain dripped from his words, "You foreigners don't know the ways of civilized people. We must remove the stench you bring."

Samson laughed. "Or calm your conscience when we stir up thoughts you don't like?"

Saraat's eyes widened, but then his face hardened. "Why should we change?"

"Because your ways do not satisfy. They do not prepare you for death."

"Who prepares for death, when life is good? Your rules bring bondage. Even your hair brings hardship. Your head must ache from carrying its weight."

It was Samson's turn for surprise. Isn't that what his *ima* had told him years ago? Perhaps that was why he suffered from headaches. But how did Saraat know that rule?

Saraat laughed. "Surprised you? It only took a meager bribe from someone in your village for them to tell all about your angel and your hair."

Samson swallowed. How easy it was for even his own to betray him. Though this betrayal was easier to accept than Tia's. Hadn't his people already showed their hatred toward his mother?

He swallowed. Saraat's ploy to distract would bring carelessness and haste.

Samson refocused, adjusting his grip and stepping forward to thrust. "Rules bring bondage only to those who follow the rules without knowing the Rule Giver. But no rule of God's is bondage when done for His pleasure."

Saraat confidently countered with his dagger. "I do nothing that does not please me."

Samson again stepped inward, pointing his dagger at Saraat's chest.

Saraat brushed it away, but not without receiving a slice on his inner arm. Blood instantly formed a line. Saraat's eyes widened and he stepped back.

Samson also stepped back. "By pleasing yourself alone, you have no pleasure."

Saraat's forehead wrinkled and his hand trembled. "Our gods are pleased by what we do."

Samson laughed. "You create your gods to control the people. Do not deceive yourselves over their reality."

Saraat's body shook. He thrust forward, striking the air with short, rapid strokes.

Samson raised his arm, countering each stroke with his own

dagger. "It's only through pleasing the God Who made you that you can truly know pleasure."

Saraat's eyes spewed hate and rage. "No God will tell me what to do."

They were standing nose to nose. Neither could move.

Samson pushed against Saraat's chest with both hands, disengaging himself and quickly followed by stepping in and slicing. His blade hit his target.

Saraat's eyes widened in surprise. "Your strength is well hidden, little man. Just like your virtue of revenge. I didn't think you would really come." His face paled.

Samson sliced upward and finished the task, holding his arm steady in spite of the blood flowing down his handle and covering his hand. "My strength comes from the God you disdain. My virtue comes by desiring to please Him. You will meet Him in death."

Samson found all twenty-eight leaders who had attended his wedding feast. He wiped his dagger on the last fallen man, adjusted his cloak and hat, and made his way to the gates of the city. They were just opening.

This city would not welcome him anymore, nor would his own people.

He traveled south several days' journey, skirting cities and towns until he came to the cliffs of Etam.

It was a wild country, with few people. The rugged hills and deserted feeling suited Samson. He gathered wood and made a fire, roasting a deer he had killed.

As he waited for his meat to cook, he watched the flames and wondered what he should do next.

CHAPTER 16

The day would be hot, but for now a breeze tossed a single strand of Z'llpunith's hair that had escaped from her braid. She brushed it aside.

All the other women would already be washing their clothes at the stream.

Z'llpunith hurried. Not that she wanted their company; she tired of their petty bickering and critical attitudes.

Manoah had encouraged her, telling her that her attitude might influence them.

She doubted it. If anything, she would become as discontent as they.

She hurried only because their company was a welcome distraction from thinking about Samson.

She shifted her basket of clothes on her hip as she reached the stream and dropped the basket beside her sister. "Shalom, Renata."

Her sister nodded. She had already started on her own overflowing basket. Renata stopped pounding a soiled spot in her husband's tunic. "You're late."

Z'llpunith could feel her cheeks flush. She bit back her reply and nodded, settling down beside her. Her basket of clothes never as full as the other women's, only reminded her that her family was less blessed. She lowered her head and worked without speaking, trying not to feel the unspoken rebuke of the others.

Another woman spoke as she wrung out a wet tunic. "My husband came back from visiting relatives in Lehi." She looked at Z'llpunith, her expression telling more than her words. "The Philistines have gone to war."

Renata sighed. "At least they aren't bothering us."

Z'llpunith bit her tongue. She knew the Philistines had not raided because of Samson. But her people would never admit it.

The way the woman kept looking at her concerned Z'llpunith. "Why did they go to war?"

Renata seemed oblivious to the undercurrent between the two women. "Do the Philistines need a reason to torment us?"

The other woman shook out her tunic and laid it on a rosemary bush where the sun would dry it and the oil would leave a pleasant smell. "The leaders from Lehi met with the Philistine leaders. They said they wanted no war, only Samson."

Z'llpunith gasped. "But they are our own people!"

The woman seemed to delay long enough to ensure every woman was listening. "The leaders of Lehi told the Philistines they would bring him, if the Philistines would promise to leave their city alone."

Z'llpunith could not believe what she was hearing. They would give one of their own to the enemy? She felt ill. Leaving her wash behind, she ran home.

She could hear the women tut-tutting behind her.

She did not care.

Z'llpunith told Manoah that evening what she had heard. "What can we do?"

"Nothing." Manoah sipped his tea. "If I tried to warn him, I'd be too late. Knowing our son, he already knows."

"But should our own people turn him over to our enemy?"

Manoah sighed. "They save their own city. They hold no loyalty to Samson."

"But shouldn't they?"

Manoah pushed his empty vessel aside and reached for Z'llpunith's hand. "He married a Philistine. As far as our people are concerned, he's one of them."

"But he's our son."

Manoah gentled his tone. "And the Lord is still with our son."

"Is He?"

"Didn't God use him with his wager? And that news about Timnah's leaders all being killed sounded like Samson. Besides . . . can we do anything about it?"

Z'llpunith shook her head. "That is why I weep."

Manoah squeezed her hand. "God will use this to show His power."

Z'llpunith wiped her eyes. "But we just wait?"

Manoah nodded, "And pray."

"And pray," Z'llpunith whispered, even though she wasn't sure how much that helped.

S amson hid for weeks in the caves, going to Lehi when he was tired of his own cooking. He was conspicuous even in Lehi because of his seven braids of hair that fell below his waist.

He moved the snared rabbit that was cooking over the fire. He hated burnt meat. He would rather eat it raw than burnt. Living in Timnah had spoiled him against his own cooking. Their meat had melted in his mouth. He tried to replicate the process, but it never seemed the same.

Maybe the rabbit was too lean or ancient. This meat would be the first cooked meal in several days.

A commotion down the hillside brought him to the cave's mouth. He listened in its shadows.

"Samson!"

His own people looked armed for battle.

Samson whistled under his breath. He called to them, "Are we going to battle?"

One man stepped forward, searching the hillside for Samson. He seemed to be the spokesman. "Samson, what have you done to us?"

This gathering was about what he'd done in Timnah? A city could not live long without someone's rules. Without those former leaders imposing their wishes, mob rule reigned until someone rose to control the people by what *he* wanted. And whoever it was who had taken over apparently wanted revenge.

Samson answered cockily. "As they did to me, so I have done to them."

The leader shook his head, his anger visible to Samson. "We've come to give you to the Philistines." He hastily added. "We will only bind you and give you to them."

Samson spoke under his breath, "As if that's any different than killing me." This was certain death, after torture. He looked around the cave. Now that his own knew where he was, he could not hide, nor could he run from a group that big. Samson would not fight his own people. He called to the leader, "I have your word, you won't kill me?"

The man visibly sighed, the tension leaving his body. "You do."

Samson scooped up his belt with its sheathed dagger.

He grabbed the rabbit from the embers and kicked the fire out.

The delay had burnt his meat.

He took a bite of the blackened ruins and crunched as he walked to meet the men.

They had ruined his dinner; they might as well ruin his life.

When he reached the bottom of the ravine where they waited, he laughed. He turned to the leader, "You brought an army to escort me?"

The leader only nodded.

Samson looked around the hills. "How many did you bring?"

The leader did not look at him as he mumbled, "Three thousand."

Samson whistled. "What did you expect me to do, fight you? You're my brothers!"

The leader's color paled and he swallowed but did not respond. Instead he pointed to Samson's belt. "Remove your dagger."

Samson fingered his dagger, debating the wisdom of using it now. This seemed like one of those times his *abba* had meant his anger would be wrong. He shook his head. "You would send me to the enemy unarmed?"

The man waited.

Samson repeated, "You're my brothers." But when the man continued to wait, Samson untied and dropped his belt and dagger. "Take care of them until I return for them."

The leader's rigid body relaxed with his concession. "Put your arms in front of you."

Another man stepped forward and tied his arms with a thick leather cord.

The leader inspected the knot, pulled on his arms, and nodded.

A third man stepped forward with another cord in his hands.

Samson laughed. "Not taking any chances?"

The leader nodded but did not smile. "Not when our families' lives are at stake."

"Do you think by turning me over to the Philistines, you will be safe? They never honor their word. The leaders I killed are the same as the leaders who steal your daughters. Do you know what they do to them? They become temple prostitutes. And *if* they last a year, they are sacrificed to their gods.

"Your safety is *not* secure by delivering me into their hands. Your oppression has just begun."

The leader's eyes widened as he listened, his face lost color, but he did not respond. He hesitated before motioning for Samson to move.

The men surrounded him and escorted him to Lehi.

Samson considered what awaited him. Death seemed the least of his worries.

Samson could think of no other time when he felt so alone in spite of being among brothers.

Before they reached the city, the leader directed another, "Go to the gate. Tell them to meet us out here."

Samson laughed. "Don't feel safe in their city?"

The leader did not smile. "They're still our enemy."

Samson studied the man. "You're afraid of these Philistines. Yet you know our God. What happened to the Lord's people who killed everyone in their path by His mighty Hand?"

The leader pushed Samson in front of him. "I don't know that God you speak of, but I do know the Philistines."

Samson snorted. "And that is why we're in this dilemma now, isn't it? Perhaps a look at our history may give you a glimpse of what God expects."

The leader responded, "You wonder why we don't fight for you?" He pointed his finger in Samson's face. "You marry them, then kill them, then tell *us* to look to God." He spit on him. "You deserve their revenge."

Samson swallowed the grief that suddenly erupted. He should have saved Tia. No amount of revenge could bring her back. Yet more than grief, anger surged through him. "You dare to point your finger at me when I am bound and defenseless. But my God has delivered me before, and He will deliver me again."

The Philistines started pouring out of the gates. They were armed for battle yet acted like a mob.

The leader pushed Samson with his sword. "Get going. We want no more from you."

Samson could speak of God's deliverance, but he could not summon God's power whenever he wanted it. God was the Giver, and only when He decided the time was right.

Samson faced the Philistines. He could expect no mercy. They tortured their own people. Like Tia's family. Burning a house seemed mild to what he envisioned they would do to him. He swallowed, though his mouth was dry, and walked toward them. His entire body shook.

The Philistines charged him like he was some animal. Their hooting and hollering sent shivers up his back. He saw the whites of their eyes and their gleaming teeth as they came closer to him, chanting, "We've got him!"

Samson glanced once behind him. His people had fled.

He stood alone.

The taste of burnt rabbit did nothing but make his mouth drier. He must remember raw is better than burnt—every time. He licked his lips.

His stomach growled from fasting. He wouldn't last long in any fight.

He walked toward the Philistines, keeping his shoulders back. His heart beat wildly in his chest. His legs felt like they were made of stones. He pushed his feet to move. He walked with his eyes closed, expecting them to reach him at any moment.

All hope left him.

But suddenly, Samson felt strength come upon him, just like when he had killed the lion, repaid his wager, and attacked the city leaders.

The strength gave him courage and confidence.

God *would* deliver him from their hand.

He never asked for the strength. But it always came when he had given up hope.

He strode toward them. His numbed hands tingled, not from the cord's confinement, but as if a fire had exploded within them. He gathered a deep breath, then he yanked his arms apart.

The leather cords squeaked and stretched under the strain, then broke, dropping to the ground. He wiggled his free fingers and relaxed his arms.

He instinctively reached for his belt—and recalled he had nothing to defend himself.

The sun reflected off a sun-bleached bone at the side of the road. A donkey's jawbone.

Samson picked it up and remained crouched, waiting.

The Philistines were upon him now, their height more than half his height again, their weapons drawn for battle. Their passion energized their revenge. Lust for blood gleamed in their eyes.

But what they met was not a man bound by two strong, leather cords; but a man who wielded a jaw bone like a sling, empowered by his God.

He caught the first man in the head and sent him sprawling.

The next man who pushed forward, anxious to abuse, never saw the bone before it slammed him. He fell back into two more men.

Those behind expected a man bound by two cords.

What they met was their death.

When the Philistine halted, then retreated, Samson estimated the fallen. With the donkey's jawbone, he had killed a thousand men.

He looked back to where his brothers had been.

Not one remained.

He stood alone on the plains of Lehi before the men he had slain.

He twirled in a circle, throwing the donkey's jawbone as far as he could.

His body trembled now from weakness and fatigue. He squatted to catch his breath.

He licked his lips. They were cracked and bleeding.

Stumbling up the hillside, he fell face down in the sand.

"Lord, You have given me this great deliverance. Now shall I die of thirst and still fall into the hands of these uncircumcised men?"

But just as the Lord was with Samson with the lion, the wager, and the Philistines, He remembered him now.

Samson did not know how long he lay there. Maybe he had dozed. But now, in his stupor and weakness, he heard dripping water.

Surely no water could be in this barren place. Was he dreaming?

A drop splashed his arm.

Reflexively he reached out.

He brought his hand back to his lips and licked it. He tasted the wetness, but also the salt from his skin. He tried to swallow.

Another drop splashed his face.

This was no dream.

He forced his body to respond to what his mind told it to do. Pushing his arms under him, he dragged himself toward the splash.

Water puddled in a rock's depression.

He drank. And drank. And drank.

He submerged his head, then shook it.

He lifted his head with effort, trying to find the source of this pool.

A rock had split above him. Water poured from it.

The Lord had heard his cry and given what he needed. He would live another day.

And rejoice in his God.

. . .

Z'llpunith could not help but smile as she placed the stew between Manoah and Tad. She had received news. Samson had escaped from the Philistines' hands with victory.

Manoah scooped a mouthful of stew onto his flatbread and took a bite. "I've missed this stew."

Z'llpunith shrugged. "We have more because the Philistines have not raided us."

Manoah continued to chew.

"Why don't our people see it is Samson who keeps the Philistines away?"

Manoah shrugged. "People see what they want to see."

"Now they have food; before they didn't."

Manoah paused chewing. "It is a dangerous thing to attribute the Lord's work to our son."

Z'llpunith could feel the color drain from her face. "But without Samson . . ."

"God would have raised up another." Manoah kept his eyes on his meal. "Z, I am proud of what Samson did. But the Lord enabled him, and that is what we should remember."

"But aren't you angry that our people turned him over to the Philistines?"

Manoah drank from his vessel. His tone was comforting but correcting, "Z, they know what the Philistines will do to their families if they don't submit."

"But if they would have helped Samson, they could have taken the city."

Manoah shrugged. "Perhaps. But God protected Samson."

She took a bite, not tasting it. "When will they acknowledge that God is using Samson? They give no praise to God. How long will God allow them to ignore His works?"

Manoah took another bite and chewed. "The Lord doesn't shout His accomplishments. He waits for His people to acknowledge them."

Z'llpunith tore her flatbread into bite-sized pieces. "What if they don't?"

Manoah grunted. "We lose. It's when we give God the praise that is due Him we feel His care and love. By ignoring Him, we forget He even cares."

"Can't we make people see?"

"Can we make a blind man see stars? He sees only darkness. To see the stars, he must have eyes that see the light. Our people only see darkness because they're not looking for God. And so He won't be found. They must *want* to see the light."

Z'llpunith mumbled. "Seems obvious to me."

"Samson's a loner. He's not a leader like Joshua who led our people into our land. Samson shows our people what God does with one man."

Z'llpunith played with the flatbread pieces. She wasn't hungry anymore. "It'd be nice if they at least helped him."

"He wouldn't want their help."

"It'd make me feel better."

Manoah rested his hand over hers and waited for her to look at him. "God doesn't do things to make you feel better."

Z'llpunith sighed, "I know."

Manoah leaned forward and kissed her. "He does things for His glory. That's where our focus should be. When we do, what others do or don't do won't bother us."

CHAPTER 17

EIGHTEEN YEARS LATER

S amson roamed the country, traveling south. The hills and caves provided him food and shelter. He lived a wild life with few comforts and less human interaction. When he approached a city, he did so with more caution than when he stalked a lion. His reputation of his ability to avenge preceded him.

His seven long locks of hair identified him to everyone. He was known, not only among his own people, who avoided him as if he had leprosy, but among the Philistines, especially the Gazites where he went for supplies. Most kept away from him, and he preferred that.

He was pulling a quail from his snare when the messenger found him.

"Your father is dying."

"Dying?" Samson looked at the messenger blankly. His father was the only one who understood him, who recognized his need for solitude, and who accepted that he must live with the Philistines.

Samson turned from the messenger to hide his grief.

The messenger hesitantly added, "He asks for you." He waited. "Your *ima* also asks for you. Do you want to send a message?"

When Samson did not answer, the. Messenger slipped quietly away.

Samson was not ready to return home.

He could ignore his people's haughty looks and comments. Even

Tad, in the few times Samson had returned home over the years, disdained him.

Samson maintained a distance. Not out of fear, but from territorial respect. Tad would care for their father's land.

Samson had no right to it. Nor did he want it.

He paused as he plucked the quail and glanced toward the city of Gaza. He hadn't been to any city in a long time. Perhaps a visit would provide answers about going home. He tossed the quail into the bushes and prepared his mouth for something better.

When he entered the city, the marketplace was bustling. The noise was loud compared to the solitude he had enjoyed.

After bartering for a roasted chicken, he stood in the shadows of a doorway eating the drumstick. It had been slow-cooked over mesquite wood. Better than he could have cooked it. After devouring it, he tossed the bones into the middle of the street and licked his fingers.

A woman bartering with a merchant caught his attention.

Her face spoke of a rough life. But her silk head covering and richly woven cloak told of paid wealth.

"No, no, no." She shook her finger in the merchant's face. "These eggs are worth only a pittance. And that's all I will give you."

The merchant watched others walk away, his possible sales with them. He took the coins she offered, shaking his head. "They are worth so much more."

She tucked the eggs under a blanket in her basket. Her bowed head did not hide her smile of victory.

She caught Samson's eye and flashed a smile that chased away some of the lines from her face.

He stepped from the shadows and fell in step beside her.

"You are not from around here."

Samson shrugged. "I go where I need to go."

She shifted her basket so she would walk closer to him. She looked directly at him. "Where do you need to go?"

Samson laughed. "Probably not with you."

She tilted her head, coyly. "But you want to be."

He shrugged. "And you read minds?"

"Only minds searching for answers."

Samson laughed. "You know the questions?"

She laughed. "You have come to the right person."

His heart skipped a beat. It was just like Tia's laugh. She also asked probing questions. His pain had softened over the years, and now he remembered only Tia's beauty and his loss.

The woman drew his attention back to the present. "What you wish is what I'll give."

B ut Samson was not the only one who watched from the shadows of the merchants' stalls. Another had followed Samson from the gate of the city. He had been too young to meet Samson when he had killed the men of Lehi with a jawbone. But he had searched the plains of Lehi for his brother to bury him. And he had hounded Samson, these last many years for a chance to avenge his brother.

When he had first seen Samson, he was surprised. Hearing of Samson's feats of strength, he had expected a big, strong man! But Samson was smaller than he was.

The watcher hated him more for his strength.

But he would not underestimate him now.

He retraced his steps to the city gate and waited in line to be heard by the city leaders. He fidgeted. His case was important. He listened as the other cases were judged. Such trivial squabbles between neighbors and families!

The sun grew hot.

The line dwindled.

The leader finally pointed to him. "What is it?"

He stepped forward, confident of his reception. "I bring news of one who will cause your city harm."

"You know this because—"

He stuttered now that he was questioned. "This man was bound by fresh cords, two of them, and brought to be judged for killing our leaders. He broke the cords as if they were nothing and killed a thousand of our soldiers. His actions bring destruction wherever he goes. He's now in this city."

Another leader added. "I've heard of him—Samson, wasn't it? He killed all the leaders of Timnah, didn't he?"

The man nodded.

"And burned their fields with foxes."

The main leader turned to the spy. "Where is he?"

The spy was smug and confident. "With a harlot."

The leader nodded. "We'll wait at the city gates. In the morning, when he leaves, we'll have him."

A detachment of extra guards was assigned at the gate for the morning watch.

The man left, rubbing his hands. He would finally have his revenge.

D uring the night, the woman's musical laugh had started to irritate Samson.

He had expected Tia's sensitive, caring interest.

This woman had a nosy, intrusive manner.

Rather than share his heart, he raised his guard.

But she had fulfilled one need.

Now when he woke in the middle of the night, he stretched. He felt trapped, uneasy. Was it because he was not used to city noises? Or that he must go home?

Whatever it was, he must leave—now.

Without waking the woman, he tied on his belt and dagger, threw on his cloak and left.

The streets, empty now, were dark, illuminated by a full moon that penetrated only the center of the streets.

Samson kept to the shadows.

The cool air invigorated him.

The gates would be closed.

One sentry would guard the bar of the gate.

That would be his only obstacle.

He paused, reaching the open courtyard where the leaders judged during the day. The moon flooded the open area with light. Skirting the area, he approached the gate in the shadows.

A cough alerted Samson.

He ducked into a doorway to appraise the situation.

Not one guard, but four stood at the gate.

The cough had been from one of them. They weren't masking their presence, so apparently they had not seen him.

Samson found six others. Two in doorways. Three leaning against the wall. Not a good way to stay alert.

The moonlight reflected off the breast plate of another.

Samson had missed that one.

He shifted from the doorway to the darkest shadow and followed the wall to the doorway where the nearest soldier waited.

Samson circled the man's neck with his arm and squeezed.

The man gasped.

Samson thrust his dagger through him, quieting him.

Samson helped him crumble to the ground, without noise, then released him.

One down.

He studied the next doorway.

Another soldier stepped out of it. "I don't see why we must guard the gate all night. If he's with the harlot, he'll be there till morning."

Others laughed.

"I've heard he's strong—nothing has ever held him."

Another, whom Samson hadn't seen, boasted, "That's because I didn't tie the knots."

While they talked, Samson slipped to the next doorway. He took care of the soldier leaning there.

His armor clanked loudly as he fell to the stone street.

"Everything all right, there?" Another called.

Samson slid across the street to where the speaker stood. This one stood more in the moonlight.

The man faced him, unsheathing his sword.

The tight space was meant for daggers and knives, not clumsy swords.

As the man raised his sword, Samson stabbed him. He whispered, "A word of advice: never expose your heart."

The sword fell from the man's hand and clattered to the cobblestones.

The noise seemed loud in the black quiet.

Samson retreated into the shadows and waited.

"Who's there?" Another solder stepped hesitantly toward where Samson waited. He tripped over the prone soldier.

Samson stabbed with his dagger, twisting deeply, then stepped back to regain his cover.

Four more came toward him.

He threw his dagger at the first who caught it in his neck.

His face registered surprise before he crumbled.

Samson grabbed his boot knife.

As he straightened, another sliced with his sword glazing his shoulder.

Samson winced, but instead of withdrawing, he stepped forward and jabbed the man under his arm. Samson whispered in the man's face as he dug his knife deeper, "The knife always wins in close quarters."

The man sank to the street.

Samson surveyed the street for others.

There were none.

Samson stepped over the bodies toward the gate. He knelt to retrieve his dagger from the soldier's neck and wiped it on the man's tunic before replacing it in his sheath.

He lifted the bar of the gate from its place and dropped it in its holding place for the day.

The clank of wood against metal seemed loud in the night's silence.

He pushed the doors open.

They squeaked on heavy hinges.

In the skirmish, he'd had no time to think.

Now he did.

They knew he was in the city.

They had tried to capture him.

Why?

The more Samson considered, the angrier he became.

He would not just leave the city. He would show them their city could not contain him.

The Lord's strength came upon him as with the lion, the wager, and the jawbone.

He leaned on the footings of the gate's pillars. The left side wobbled. The wall around the pillars crumbled and the rocks shifted. Some rolled to the ground.

He pushed on the right side until it, too, was loose.

He wiped his hands on his cloak.

Leaning into the center of the gate, he heaved himself against its weight.

A crack pierced the night's silence as the wooden framework split and shifted away from the stone wall that supported it.

Stumbling forward to catch his footing, he braced himself, adjusting the gate's weight on his shoulders.

Behind him, the wall creaked, shifted, and tumbled to the ground, blocking the entrance.

Samson took a moment. He was outside the city.

No one would confine him!

The gate was solid wood. Built to keep the city safe.

Now no one would feel safe.

Instead of discarding the gate outside the city, he carried it. The hill's momentum enabled him to run to the bottom of the valley.

When he reached the bottom, he looked to the crest of the next hill and chuckled. He would do it.

He shifted his hold and trudged up the hill. With each step, he grunted and breathed deeply. Sweat poured from his face down his arms and back and drenched his clothes.

At the top of the hill overlooking the city, he pushed the gate from his back.

It crashed to the ground. The sound echoed across the night hills.

He wiped his forehead. Brushing splinters from his cloak, he looked back at the city's entrance, now a mound of rubble.

He would never know what the city had planned for him.

But he did acknowledge the Lord's strength to allow his escape.

. . .

The sun cast its shadows as if it mourned the day's endings. A warm breeze swept across the fields, promising another hot day on the morrow. The rains had come and with it a good barley harvest. The fields lay dormant,awaiting another planting. Tad watched the lone figure approach. "You could have come sooner."

Samson shrugged. "I was busy."

Tad wiped his hands down his tunic. "*Abba* could have used your help."

Samson did not like being pressed. "You helped, and I thank you."

"He asked for you."

Samson tilted his head, "How's *Ima*? Are you taking care of her?"

"Better than you."

Samson smiled for the first time. "Good."

They walked together in a silent, resigned truce to the house.

Samson eyed the crowd of family and villagers who mingled inside and outside of their house. He kept himself apart but watched. He made eye contact with his *ima*.

Her eyes were red and swollen. She approached him.

When Samson hugged her, she seemed slim and frail.

She tried to smile. It was wobbly. Her voice broke. "He asked for you. He told me to tell you, 'You are not alone.'"

Samson swallowed, feeling the need to hold onto her. Alone was what he seemed always to be. He squeezed her gently. "How was he—at the end?"

She wiped her eyes. "He was the only one who understood you. He knew what you needed."

Samson nodded. He would be missed.

His *ima* was still talking. "You wouldn't have recognized him. I had to feed him . . . . He was ready to go."

The funeral for Manoah lasted several days.

Day followed day. After a week, Samson approached his *ima*.

Before he could say anything, she held up her hand. "I see it in your eyes. You're leaving."

Samson started to explain but shut his mouth. What could he say?

She held his arm. "Do one thing for me."

Samson inwardly sighed. She had that look of a request he would not like.

"Consider one of our own girls for a wife. You will be lonely."

"*Ima*—"

"When your strength gives way, you will still have years to live. You won't want to live alone."

He swallowed a harsh retort about their people.

As if hearing his thoughts, she continued, "I know our people didn't treat you right, but there are good girls here—"

Samson hugged her. "I must go, *Ima*. I'll visit again."

"About my request?"

"I'll think about it."

She laughed, "Which means you'll humor me until you leave."

Samson squeezed her tightly. "You could always read my thoughts. I can't stay."

She swallowed and nodded.

Samson found Tad in the barn. "I'm going." He shifted his feet and nodded toward the house. "Thanks for taking care of *Ima*."

Tad's face was hard. "Someone had to. She fell apart when *Abba* died."

Samson turned to leave but gestured toward the pastures. "You've done well."

"Father needed a son who would take care of them in their old age. God gave them one."

Samson swallowed. "So He did."

CHAPTER 18

After leaving his own village, Samson traveled south. From a hillside, he surveyed a small Israelite village. He carried an offering of a fresh-killed deer over his shoulders. The field below was stubble, blackened by the fires of some Philistine raid. An older man with what looked like his daughters was planting.

Samson shifted the deer on his shoulders and hiked down to their field. Dropping the meat in the shade of a tree, he nodded to the man, who merely looked up at his greeting. He removed his cloak, rubbed his hands on his tunic, and stepped into the field toward one of the women. "I can help."

The woman continued as if he had not said anything.

He spoke louder. "I can help."

She gestured by a slight nod toward the man.

Samson felt his face flush. He had grown accustomed to the forwardness of the Philistine women and had forgotten his people allowed no man to speak to a woman directly.

Though rebuffed by the man, he must go through him. His people, with their unspoken rules! He turned again to the man who watched him. "I'd like to help. May I?"

The man gave a slight nod, then continued across the field.

The woman removed the seed bag and extended it to Samson. "Thank you. It's heavy."

Samson swung it over his shoulder and continued across the field, casting the seed into the blackened soil.

She walked with him a few steps.

"The venison is for your family. If you want it."

She finally looked at his face and smiled. "That would be a welcome change."

When the day finished, the meal was eaten in silence. They did not offer him a bed in their barn, so he slept on the hills outside their village.

He stayed several weeks, finishing their planting and helping with their flocks.

Their responses were forced and rigid. The entire community avoided him. When they saw him walking down the only street in their village, they crossed to the other side to avoid him.

What had he done to merit this? How was he to honor his *ima's* request, when they would not even talk with him?

The entire village joined together for the grape harvest.

It was hot, sticky work, bending under the grape vines to cut and collect the fruit into baskets.

Two men carried the baskets to vats for winemaking.

No one helped Samson with his basket. He struggled under its weight. When he heard several of them talking as he reached the end of the row where others had gathered, he slowed his steps.

"People say he moved a city gate. They lie."

"He can hardly lift the baskets of grapes!"

Samson dropped his basket and wiped his hands down his tunic, their stickiness forgotten. Is that what people thought? They expected him to perform for their amusement?

The Lord's strength did not come upon him when he wished it, only when the Lord wanted it.

Another criticized. "Who'd believe a Gazite anyway?"

"He's a drifter, irresponsible. Didn't he leave his aging parents, in order to roam the countryside?"

"He didn't return when his father was dying."

Samson surveyed the faces before him. He could not follow his *ima*'s wishes to marry a daughter from his own people. They would never understand or accept him.

Nor would he try any more.

He backed away unnoticed, circled the group and the tables loaded with food for their celebration of harvest, and left.

He would miss the food and wine.

But he would not miss anything else.

S amson lived in the hill country of Sorek, surviving on the trapped animals that preyed on pastures and orchards. But the time in the village had awakened a thirst for companionship.

His *ima* probably was right. He did yearn for someone who would understand and accept him.

His loneliness escalated. He did not like that he needed anyone, yet he remembered his parent's companionship and wished for someone who would respect him for who he was, not for what he could do.

He traveled farther one morning, tracking signs of bigger game than the quail he normally ate. At the crest of the hill, he surveyed the scene below.

A house lay tucked in the valley. A well-made barn was surrounded by corrals loaded with goats. Two women separated the bucks from the nannies.

Castrating was miserable work. A good buck could support forty does. The young bucks not showing promise would be culled for meat or sold.

The goats looked of excellent quality.

The women more so.

Samson made his way down the hillside. When he came within speaking distance, he remembered his former mistake and addressed the man. He nodded toward the separated bucks. "Want help?"

The man glanced at his herd, then at Samson.

Samson felt his scrutiny. He smiled as he extended the quail. "Perhaps this may add to your dinner."

The man tucked the quail under his cloak and nodded to the corrals. "Perhaps."

"I am Samson."

The man extended his hand. "I know. I am Abaddon."

S amson entered the corral. The smell reminded him of why he had never enjoyed herding his father's goats. Bucks in rutting season urinate into their mouths, chest, face, and beard, turning their hair yellow. The smell brought the does into heat.

Samson moved among the yearlings as they butted one another for dominance. Their horns clanked loudly over their bleating.

These had been culled for future breeding none too soon. Since they had entered the rutting season, some would be injured if left together.

Samson looked over the corrals and sighed. Why had he volunteered?

He grabbed one goat, flipping it over and straddling it, even as he unsheathed his knife.

A voice at his elbow gave him pause, "I've got him, if you'd cut."

He looked up from the goat into eyes clear as blue water.

From the hillside, this daughter seemed only a girl, but looking into her eyes, Samson realized she was no more a girl than he just a boy.

The goat slipped from his hand.

She laughed.

Not the sound of music like Tia, but still a laughter that bubbled from within.

She pointed to the goat who now hid among the others. "He'll be doubly hard to catch again."

Samson's eyes followed her finger. "It was worth it."

She grabbed another buck.

Her movements brought Samson back to what he should do. He flipped the goat and straddled it.

She calmed it, stroking its face. "Thunder, that's enough."

Samson was drawn to look into those eyes again. "It has a name?"

She rewarded him with another laugh. "They all do. Shouldn't we enjoy the memories they leave in this life?"

Samson nodded. "And what memory would life hold of you?"

She bowed her head. "I'm just a goat herder."

Samson performed the needed cut.

She held a vessel toward him.

He dug his fingers into the thick salve and smeared it on the incision. Blood coated his hand, as the goat squirmed under the application. He looked back into her eyes. "Even a goat herder deserves a name."

"I am Deliliah."

"The memory of a certain goat herder by the name of Deliliah will be etched in my mind."

"And who is the man who touches my father's goats with skill, yet acts like he would rather be anywhere else?"

Samson laughed. "This was the job I hated most with my father's goats."

"But you volunteered now?"

"I saw you."

"You still have not told me your name."

"Samson."

"I've heard of you. The wild man with long hair who wrecks cities that he enters."

It was Samson's turn to look down.

"Yet," she continued, "you have a gentleness with my father's goats that speaks of kindness and tenderness."

Samson felt his face flush. Her words soothed the deep wounds caused by his own people.

Without embarrassing him anymore, she pointed to another goat. "Grumpy will be next."

The sun rose higher in the sky. The day grew hot. And still they worked.

Samson's appreciation for her increased as the day wore on.

When the last goat was finished, he looked over the corral. "I'm curious."

"Yes?"

"When I watched from the hillside, I saw two women. Why are you chosen to work the goats?"

"You watched us?"

"To make sure it was safe."

"Safe?" She watched him. "What danger did you think we would cause you?"

"My life's been saved many times by first looking for danger."

Her eyes sparkled. "Sounds like stories I'd love to hear."

They walked toward the house.

She scrubbed her hands, arms, and face with the soap and water by the house. "I don't relish smelling of goat through dinner, but it cannot be helped. My sister should thank you personally for doing her job for her. But she is nowhere to be seen."

Samson dipped his head into the vessel. His hair shed the water when he took it out. He ran his hands through his seven long tresses before scrubbing his face, arms, and hands with soap. "I should thank her. For without her absence, I wouldn't have worked with you." His eyes met hers.

She blushed and looked down. "It's unusual Father allowed a stranger to touch his beloved goats."

Samson took the linen towel and wiped a drip of water from her nose. "I should thank him as well."

She stared into his face.

"Who are we having for dinner, Deliliah?"

The voice startled them.

Deliliah looked down. "A guest welcomed by Father. This is my sister, Chittem. This is Samson."

The newcomer's laughter did not hold the sincerity of Deliliah's.

Samson nodded. "It's with great anticipation I await your dinner."

Chittem humphed.

Deliliah laughed outright. "Hold your appreciation until you've tasted her offerings."

"Hunger can make a man eat anything." Samson looked again at Deliliah.

She shook her head. "You might get anything. But that doesn't guarantee you can eat it."

Chittem pointed to the coals where the quail lay skewered. "Cooked meat is better than raw."

Both girls laughed. One so sincere and bubbly, the other as if in mockery to her own words.

A man's voice spoke behind them. "We'll know soon enough." Abaddon gestured to the table. "Anyone who works my goats deserves to share my table."

Samson bowed to him. "I hope I've performed to your satisfaction."

Deliliah interjected. "Father, his hands are like a physician's— precise, accurate, and gentle."

Abaddon studied Deliliah. "You've spoken high praise of our guest."

Deliliah lowered her head and blushed.

Her humility and praise endeared her to Samson. "Only because of the help by my side."

Abaddon looked sternly at Samson. "Indeed."

S amson settled into a routine. Initially he thought Abaddon did not trust him, because Deliliah was always at his side, but the more she followed him to fix fences, dam streams for watering holes, and other tasks, the more he did not think so. "Why doesn't your father hire servants for these tasks?"

She sighed. "My father treats me as his first-born son. He expects me to do the jobs."

Samson processed this information. "Why doesn't your father take more of an interest?"

She shrugged and put the rock down in the dam they were fixing. "My father once prided himself with his fine flocks and lands."

"Until?"

"My mother died."

"When was this?"

"Shortly after my sister was born. Everything fell apart. I was ten at the time. I cooked for us to survive. Though I tease my sister about her cooking, she does cook better than I. So I help with the animals."

Samson stopped working to listen. "Your father depends on you."

She shrugged. "The land is good. Others want it."

"Wouldn't it be better to sell your land so you wouldn't have to work so hard?"

Deliliah didn't say anything for a long time. "The work isn't hard. I do what I want. Where would we go, if we left our land?"

Samson understood. What would his family do without their land? "How often do the Philistine rulers bother you?"

Deliliah shrugged. "They forget about us, until they see our herds at sales."

"Are you safe?"

Deliliah laughed. "You are talking about safety again. Don't you leave a city with its gate on your back?"

"How do you know about that?"

Deliliah blushed. "We hear news from other cities, especially news so unusual." She shrugged. "My father went to the city when you first came and asked about you."

"He thought I was safe enough for you."

"He didn't believe all the stories of strength. He says you're a good man who works hard."

"You don't believe my strength?"

"You have strength for the job before you."

Her answer did not speak of condemnation and rebuke like his own people had given.

He pried his shovel under a rock.

The rock did not budge. This would require more digging.

He sighed. He wished he could prove his strength to this family.

Why did it concern him that they didn't believe?

But Samson knew the answer.

He had learned to care for Deliliah more than he wanted to admit.

CHAPTER 19

Samson and Deliliah took the culled goats to the corrals outside the city. Their sale went well. Deliliah tucked the silver carefully in the inner pocket of her tunic and patted it to make sure it was safe.

Samson looked toward the city. "I must see to some things."

Deliliah nodded. "As do I."

They entered the city together.

Deliliah made her way to the market where she hoped to find cloth for a new tunic. After Samson came, she had noticed how worn and frayed hers were.

She eyed the silks. Such finery would not last long in the barn. Still she touched the softness.

A voice behind her startled her. "We must know where Samson gets his strength."

Deliliah recognized the voice as Hadid, one of the Philistine lords. He had offered to buy her from her father, but her father had refused.

That had not stopped Hadid from hounding her whenever she came to the city. Once he had accosted her in the city's corrals. She had escaped when a messenger had interrupted. He beat the messenger as she fled.

Another time, she had not been able to run before he had taken what was not his.

Now, she lowered her head to look for help.

No one would stand against a ruler.

She clutched the silk but had lost the image of her fine garments. She whispered. "He has no strength. Why do you pursue him?"

"Don't let his manner deceive you. In his anger, he kills. And when he kills, the destruction is great."

Deliliah felt her face drain of color. Her father had told of rumors, but she could not believe them of Samson. Samson's firm but gentle manner, even with the goats, reminded her there was more to life than silver. He treated her specially, as if she had worth. She cared for Samson. She would not do it. She shook her head.

Hadid pressed, "Would 11,000 pieces of silver from each Philistine ruler help you decide?"

Deliliah gasped. That was a lot of money. She tightened her grasp on the silk material as if that could make her decide.

The merchant jabbered, "You buy or don't touch." He peeled the material from her hand and stroked it as if cleaning it from her touch.

Deliliah could wear rich finery with that money. Even sell the land and live elsewhere. Hadn't Samson suggested that very thing?

Hadid's servants dressed in silk, but at what cost? Would accepting the offer make Hadid feel entitled to her?

She moved to another merchant.

Hadid followed her. "You think Samson will keep you safe? His own wife was burned to ashes while he was away. He will leave, and then—" his pause made her cringe, "I will get what is mine."

If she refused, who would keep her safe? Her father could not even protect her against Philistine lords. And Samson was not always with her.

She felt trapped. Perhaps she could send Samson away. She bit her lip. "How should I bring word?"

"By Abaddon."

Deliliah nodded.

Deliliah felt him leave. She heaved a sigh and hurried from the silks. She glanced back several times to ensure he did not follow, finally stopping to catch her breath.

Another voice spoke behind her, "It's not the right one."

She jumped and screamed.

Samson put his hand protectively on her waist and laughed. "Sorry. I didn't mean to startle you. You seemed deep in thought over the vessel." He nodded to what she held.

Deliliah looked at the vessel. It was an ugly vessel she would never use. She put it back on the blanket and laughed, but it wasn't her genuine laugh. She wiped her hands down her tunic. But it did nothing to make her feel clean on the inside.

Her thoughts were far from jars and merchants to a place where she had fought a man's hold without success.

The memory brought fear. She would do anything to keep safe.

S amson walked as if the sun touched his feet. He whistled as Deliliah and he made their way back to her home. He had rushed his marriage to Tia in order to claim her from Lucas. But this time, he had not rushed.

Samson had worked for Abaddon long enough to test Deliliah's sincerity. Everything she did seemed to speak of truth and wholeness, even her laughter. He would not find a more trustworthy companion.

They stopped to eat under a tree. Samson drank from the stream. He dunked his face and splashed his arms, letting the cool water drip from him. He sat back on his knees and wiped his face with the sleeve of his tunic. "You've been quiet. Something wrong?"

Deliliah shrugged, then took a long drink before answering. "The culls brought a good price."

"But?"

"Ever want something badly, but you don't know if that's what you really want?"

Samson laughed. "I don't wait to wonder. I just get it."

Deliliah forced a smile. "Was it what you wanted?"

Samson's thoughts returned to Tia. "I didn't wait to marry Tia. She seemed an answer to my dreams."

Deliliah moved closer to Samson. "But you told me her family was threatened."

Samson looked pensive. "I didn't believe her."

Deliliah pushed. "And what if you did? You weren't there when she needed protection." Deliliah rested her head on Samson's shoulder. Her tone was soothing, even though her words stung.

His voice took a hard tone. "They received what was due them."

"But too late to save her."

Her words stung. They reminded him of his own regrets. Would Tia be alive still if he had believed her? Samson stood and shook the water from his hair. "I would've died protecting her."

His answer did not comfort.

Samson took her hand and helped her stand. They started back up the path. They still had a long way before reaching home.

Instead of continuing their discussion, they fell silent. Both in thoughts of their own.

The sun had fallen by the time they saw a distant light flickering from a candle in the window. Deliliah sighed. "We're home."

Samson laughed. "Sounds like you didn't expect to get home."

"Safety isn't something we are promised."

Samson smiled. "But it is something I would like to give you."

Deliliah's voice faltered as she noticed his face. "You've decided something. . ."

"Yes, I want you for my wife." He reached into his cloak's pocket and pulled out a necklace.

Even in the fading light, Samson could tell Deliliah's face lost its color. "Your father has given consent."

Deliliah withdrew her hand from his. "It's so sudden."

"Surely, you've known my intent. I wouldn't stay and castrate goats because I like to!"

"No, but. . ."

"I love you. What is left to say?"

Deliliah didn't say anything.

"Deliliah, look at me." His tone made her raise her head, but she still didn't lift her eyes. He touched her chin. "Look at me."

He saw tears. He softened his tone. "What's the matter? Don't tell me you love my best friend?"

She forced a laugh. "No, Samson. But. . ."

"There are no buts." He wiped her eyes with the tip of his finger. "I haven't misread your interest while we worked side-by-side for weeks, have I? There's no other?"

She shook her head and lowered her eyes. "Samson, please don't. . ."

"I can give you some time. Would that help?"

Deliliah shrugged, but couldn't say anything.

"Good." Samson dropped his hand. "Let's go home."

S amson leaned against Deliliah's knees and stretched out his legs toward the fire before them. "That was a good meal."

Deliliah laughed. "Quail and watercress? I've had better."

They had gathered the scattered herd and found tracks of a lion.

"You don't know how many meals I've eaten where the quail wasn't cooked and the watercress wasn't to be found."

Deliliah shivered. "Samson, always cook your meat."

"When you're hungry enough, you'll do anything."

Even if she did care for Samson, it would only be a matter of time before the rulers would harm her or her family. Yet what would happen to Samson if she betrayed him?

She must do what was best for her family. Her family could use the promised silver to make needed repairs on their house and barn. And there would be enough for her to buy that silk.

Besides Samson would always break free. Isn't that what the rumors said? He could do it again.

"Why the heavy thoughts? You've been picking at that watercress as if you expected a bug."

"Thoughts?" She laughed lightly as she resumed eating. "What would you do with 44,000 pieces of silver?"

Samson's eyebrows lifted. "That's some heavy thinking." He sat beside her. "Depends on whether there's a riddle to redeem or a payment due." He stretched his legs and leaned on his arms and looked at the clouds above.

"If there were no obligations, what would you do?"

Samson laughed. "Silver always comes with obligations. If not before, later. So, what are you doing to get that much silver?"

Deliliah laughed, but it sounded hollow even to herself. "Nothing. Just thinking."

Samson seemed to study her then. "That much money would give you a new start. You could sell the land and move to the city. But you've already told me that wouldn't be the life for you. I don't see you in fine silks either."

Deliliah felt her cheeks burn as she looked down. Could he read her mind?

"Your beauty needs no silks." He leaned forward and took her hand. "What would you do with it?"

"I would go where it was safe."

Samson dropped his teasing. "Are you in danger? By whom?"

Deliliah regretted her questions. She had let her guard down. She would always be in danger, as long as Hadid lived. She forced a smile and squeezed his hand. "It's nothing. Only a dream and a cloud." But she clung to that dream of safety and wished for a cloud of protection.

She shook her head and tried to distract with another question. "Where do you think this lion will go?"

Samson gnawed on a leg bone. "It's full, so it will head for the higher hills."

"Must we trail it?"

Samson threw the bone into the flames. It sizzled before burning. He patted her knee and sat up. "*We* will not, *I* will."

"Will you be safe?" Deliliah's voice broke.

"I told you of the lion who attacked—"

She nodded, shivering. "I don't like thinking of it. What if your strength isn't enough this time?"

"God is with me."

Deliliah leaned forward and put her arms around Samson and whispered in his ear. "What would it take to bind you so you couldn't escape?"

Samson laughed. "Nothing has caught me yet."

Deliliah tapped her fingers on his chest. "But what would?"

Samson took her fingers and kissed them. "I suppose—if someone tied me with seven fresh, green cords, I'd be so weak, I'd be like any other man."

Deliliah inhaled deeply. "Well then, I guess you'll be safe with the lion."

Samson laughed. "So I shall be."

A fter parting with Samson, Deliliah hurried home to get word to the rulers. Getting Samson to tell her of his strength had been too easy. Had he just been playing with her? Did he sense her deceit? She shook her head. She had done nothing wrong.

Yet.

When she reached the hillside that overlooked her house, she stopped. Twenty horsemen surrounded her father by their house. Hadid had not waited for her to send word. If he did not keep his word now, what made her think he would pay her?

She swallowed, looking back the way she had come.

Samson was nowhere to be seen. He could not protect her now nor always. Even if he were here, what could he do against twenty men? Isn't that what Hadid had told her?

The image of a long, flowing silk dress flashed before her eyes. She sighed.

She would choose safety.

She threw back her shoulders and approached the group.

Her father saw her coming.

His eyes softened. His shoulders relaxed. Relief spread across his features. "Here's Deliliah. I'm sure she has the information you seek."

Deliliah felt the eyes of every man as she approached. She wanted to run any direction but toward them, but she willed herself to join them.

Hadid nudged his horse toward her. His hand twitched as he held a horse whip. "What have you found?"

She shivered. Her throat felt dry. She licked her lips. Fingers squeezed her throat, choking her. How could she betray Samson?

She looked into the other men's hard, expectant faces. Then lowered her eyes. She did not recognize her own voice, "If Samson is bound with seven new, green cords, he will be weak."

Her shoulders fell. The tightness of her chest loosened, and she breathed. It had taken all she had to tell them.

Maybe Samson wouldn't return from hunting the lion. Samson could still escape. Couldn't he?

Hadid nodded to her, as if he shared a secret with her.

She cringed.

"We'll bring them at once. Others will hide until you tie him—to make sure you have spoken truth."

Deliliah stepped back. "He's not here. I don't know when he'll return." She dropped her head, realizing she had confessed she would be unprotected. If Samson didn't come back, Hadid would. And he would take what he thought was his. What had she done?

Hadid smiled, but it did not meet his eyes. "Send word through Abaddon."

Hadid hovered over her and whispered, "I'll be back. And after I take care of Samson, I'll come for you."

Deliliah trembled. What if Samson couldn't break the cords and help her?

She squeezed her eyes shut, trying to block memories of when Hadid had caught her before.

When she opened her eyes, all she saw was his retreating back as he rode away. But she knew it would not be for long.

D eliliah stood in the darkened barn doorway, looking over their pastures and up into the hills. Although it had been only a few days since Samson had left to hunt the lion, she could not wait for his return. Yet she wished he would not return. If he did not, she would not really betray him. How could she like him, yet hurt him?

Her father approached her.

She had sensed his desire to talk since the rulers had visited. Every time, she had hurried away on some pretense. Now she could not run. To speak of what she must do would feel like admitting her guilt. She hated herself for it. Why had she agreed?

His silhouette stood framed against the rising sun. "Deliliah." His tone pleaded, almost coaxing, as if speaking to one of his wounded goats.

Deliliah ran to her father's arms. "What have I done?"

He held her. "You're caught between two dangers. The rulers—they will crush you if you don't help them. And Samson—" he left his sentence hanging. Neither one of them had witnessed his supposed strength. Could he protect them against so many?

T he lion had covered some distance between killing the goat and settling down to sleep. And so Samson had been far over the hills before he had found the lion. He had taken the choice pieces of the lion with him. It would be good to have a good cooked meal.

Before descending the hill, Samson studied the house and barn. It was a habit. It kept him alive. He sighed. From the hillside, he saw Deliliah bringing straw into the barn.

But more than that, he longed to know Deliliah was fine. Her questions about safety worried him. There was something she was not telling him.

He adjusted his water skin and shifted the pelt over his shoulder.

When he reached the barn, he dropped the skin and meat outside the door so the animals would not be unsettled by the scent of blood, and entered. His steps made no noise as he walked behind Deliliah and placed his arms around her. "I have come for you."

Deliliah screamed and thrashed.

Samson had only meant to hug her. Why such a response? He raised his voice, "Deliliah! It's me."

His voice seemed to penetrate her panic. She stopped fighting and turned in his arms. "Oh, Samson, why did you return?"

He laughed. "You didn't want me to?"

"I thought maybe the lion would . . ." she couldn't finish her sentence.

He held her tighter. "That lion won't bother your flocks anymore."

Later when they were eating, Samson embellished the story of the hunt to get a response from Deliliah, but she seemed preoccupied.

Samson pushed from his place and stretched his legs. "That meal was delicious, Chittem."

Deliliah refilled his tea and her father's wine.

Abaddon shook his head. "No more for me."

Samson looked again at Abaddon. Normally he would relax after eating. "Did anything happen while I was gone?"

All three looked down.

To Samson, it felt like the silence before the lion's attack. Silence spoke. Danger was coming. He shrugged it off. How could it, here among friends?

Abaddon pushed from the table. "I'm tired. I think, I'll go to bed."

Chittem stood, almost immediately. "Me, too."

When they were alone in the room, Samson brought Deliliah to his side. "What is it?"

"Nothing." But she said it in haste, as if she hid something.

Rather than pursue it, Samson asked, "Did anyone visit?" He said it in jest, for who would visit?

Her eyes widened and she stammered.

Samson brought his face closer to hers and laughed. "Deliliah, you act like someone did. Who?"

She shook her head and did not meet his eyes. "Let's not talk about what happened while you were gone. I'm glad you returned."

Samson squeezed her. "Fine. But I'd like to know what has caused you to be so skittish. You're worse than a heifer about to calve."

But she would not answer him.

The evening passed. Samson yawned and stretched. "You have spoiled me with cooked meals and soft beds. While I was gone, all I could think of was what I had left behind."

Deliliah stroked his hair. "Go to sleep, Samson. You are home now."

Deliliah dared not breath as Samson relaxed with his head on her lap.

Samson was a light sleeper.

She feared her nervousness might waken him. She waited. Her legs fell asleep where his head rested. She wanted to wiggle her toes to bring back circulation, but she dared not.

When Samson's breathing became deep and rhythmic, she reached under the cushions and pulled out the seven fresh, green cords.

Samson stirred and chewed in his sleep.

She waited until he resumed his heavy breathing. She brought his hands together and wrapped the cord around them and pulled it tight with a knot.

She released a breath.

Now for the hard part.

She coughed. A signal to those who waited in the inner room.

She felt, rather than heard the door behind her open.

She cleared her throat. Then yelled, "Samson!"

He jumped to his feet, instantly awake. The cords she had tightly and securely tied, snapped as he reached for his dagger, and unsheathed it. "What is it, Deliliah?"

She reminded herself to close her mouth. Those cords fell from his wrists as if they were grass!

He saw the Philistines; then his eyes fell back on her.

She lowered her own and felt color rush to her face.

The men rushed at him, expecting a captured victim.

Samson stepped between Deliliah and them.

The first man's eyes widened as he saw Samson face him with a dagger. He hesitated, but was pushed from behind by another.

Samson knifed him, withdrew his dagger, and sliced the next man. Before the men knew what was happening, Samson had killed them.

All except one.

Hadid had been in the rear of the group. He watched each man fall. Rather than advance, he had backed away.

Now Samson stepped over the other men and faced Hadid.

Hadid's eyes widened, and his face took on a deathly hue.

Samson lowered his arm. "I will allow you to return to the city and warn those who would try this again."

Hadid took a deep breath. His color returned and with it a hardness. Before he left, he glared at Deliliah. His eyes revealed hatred, revenge, and ownership.

Deliliah could not breathe. Samson was still free! Samson had killed them all.

All but the one who needed killing.

Samson sheathed his dagger. "What was that all about?"

How could she look into his trusting face again? She shrugged. "An unexpected visit?"

Samson nodded in disbelief.

Chittem and Abaddon had returned during the struggle.

Samson pointed to the floor filled with bodies. "Sorry about the mess."

Abaddon nodded. "You have protected my house. I am grateful."

Chittem stepped over the bodies and touched Samson's arm. "No, Father, he protected his own life." She glared at Deliliah.

Samson picked up the frayed pieces of cord and handed them to Deliliah.

She grabbed them as if they were her life. Samson had been spared. But at what cost?

Samson walked out the door.

Deliliah followed him. "Samson! Wait! Where are you going?"

"I'm tired. I'll sleep in the barn."

"Oh." Deliliah gulped back her relief.

Coldness crept over her. Would he leave? What would happen when Hadid returned? She ran after him. Her excuses sounded small even to her. "Samson, you weren't here to protect me—"

Samson nodded without turning around. "Of course. It's all about safety, isn't it?"

Deliliah grabbed his arm. "You can be angry about what I did, but you lied to me. You didn't tell me where your strength was."

Samson pushed her hand off his arm. "And if I had, where would I be?"

Deliliah stammered. "He would have hurt me."

"So, you betray me?" Samson entered the barn and disappeared into its darkness.

She stared after him. The blackness oozed around her until it choked her. It was one thing to convince herself this was right when Samson wasn't here and she felt unsafe. But how could she convince her heart this was right when he looked so hurt by what she had done?

She slumped against the doorway of the barn. She would stay here all night to make sure he did not leave.

The coldness of the ground and the night's air seeped over her, but it was not as strong as the coldness of her hatred for her own self. How could she have betrayed someone she loved?

Hadid's face came to mind. The fear it brought made her wonder, What would Hadid do to her when he returned after being made a fool?

She preferred staying close to Samson. At least Samson said he loved her.

Although Samson had told Deliliah he was tired, and he was, when he lay in the pile of straw, he could not sleep. He heard Deliliah settle at the barn door. He smiled. That would not keep him from leaving if he wanted. But he wasn't sure he wanted to. He would not run away like he had with Tia. By running that first time, he had lost Tia. Now what should he do? He had proclaimed his love and intention of marriage. It was Deliliah who had hesitated. Was this the cause of her apparent fear?

Deliliah had given him no answers. He would get them from Abaddon. With that resolution, he made a comfortable spot in the hay and slept.

In the middle of the night, he awakened, poked by some piece of straw. He grabbed a blanket kept in the barn for warming kids chilled at birth. He was almost asleep again when he heard a scream.

"Don't touch me!"

He ran to where Deliliah was, still blocking the doorway.

She was asleep.

He picked her up and held her close. "Shhh. There now. You were dreaming. I've got you."

She grabbed him as if she would not let go. Her body was cold. He could feel her heart beating wildly against his chest, her breathing labored.

He took her back to the hay and held her until she settled into a restful sleep. He covered her with the barn blanket and moved to the doorway.

In the morning, he awoke feeling someone watch him. He opened one eye and saw Deliliah leaning over him.

She smiled. "Morning."

He opened both eyes. "Indeed. It is morning." He wanted to ask about her nightmares and the Philistines, but thought better of it when he saw her smiling.

CHAPTER 20

Deliliah changed before his eyes from the calm, confident treasure to a groveling, desperate beggar. Day after day, she begged him to be tell where his strength lay. Sometimes she cried; other times acted coy. Her eyes lost their sparkle; they held a haunted look, as if someone was pursuing her. She never let him out of her sight, even if he needed to check herds far from home. She clung to him, as if by his presence the evil would be kept away.

Her nagging reminded him of another who had begged out of fear. Because of him, she had lost her life. He would not leave again.

Often in the night, Samson heard her screams, but by day she would not reveal the reason.

One afternoon, while Delilah was washing clothes, Samson slipped from her side to find Abaddon, fixing a latch for a gate.

Samson leaned on the fence. "You know I love your daughter. I would do anything to protect her."

Abaddon's hands paused in his work.

"Who threatens your family?"

Abaddon looked up from his work. "When my wife died, I couldn't save her. I was helpless as I watched her die." He sighed as if the grief would overtake him now, years later. "My daughters are all I have." His voice broke. "I don't know what I would do without them."

Samson wanted to shake him, but he restrained himself. "Who threatens them?"

Abaddon shook his head. "Nothing can be done."

Samson looked at Abaddon's dejected form and stormed over the hillside. He would get no answers from him.

When he reached the top, rather than silhouette himself at the top, he skirted down the other side to some boulders. He studied the pastures below him. One of Abaddon's herds grazed below.

They had separated the goats from the sheep and moved the ewes closer to the barn for lambing.

Because Deliliah had been so skittish, Samson had recommended a neighbor boy watch the flocks.

The boy was now directing one goat away from the flock toward some boulders. His movements seemed peculiar.

Movement behind the boulders caught Samson's eye.

Someone was there.

The boy stood still, as if listening, then shook his head. He seemed to take something from the one behind the boulders and put it in his cloak pocket. Then returned the goat to the flock.

In a few moments, a horse and rider cantered up the opposite hillside. The rider's face was shadowed by his hood, but his cloak was of rich weave and the horse of good stock.

When the horse and rider were no longer visible, Samson made his way toward the field.

The boy stuck his hand in his pocket and mumbled a greeting.

"What you were paid to do?"

The boy looked quickly at the hillside where the horseman had disappeared.

Samson grabbed the boy's hand and yanked it from his pocket.

A silver piece dropped at his feet.

Samson nodded toward the boulders. "Who paid you?

The boy stepped back and stammered. "My brother."

Samson grabbed the boy by his cloak and shook him. "Your family has a horse of that quality? Do not lie to me. Who was it?"

The boy's face grew ashen. "I'm paid to watch goats, not answer your questions."

Samson let go of the boy. "So, if I paid you, like that horsemen, you'd answer my questions?"

The boy looked down. "No, that's not what I meant."

Samson swallowed. Showing his anger would not give him answers. He turned as if to go, but after taking a few steps, turned back. "Who is he?"

The boy had not moved. His hand clenched his staff. His knuckles showed white. "I cannot tell."

Samson bit back his frustration. "Can't or won't?"

The boy's tone was pleading. "For the safety of my family, I can't."

Samson blew out a deep breath. Safety again.

Who did these people fear?

When Samson returned to the yard after speaking with the herdsman, he had a plan.

Deliliah ran and embraced him. "Samson! I couldn't find you. I thought you had left."

Samson held her. "I'm here."

He led her to the house and held the dipper for her. "Drink."

She gulped down the water, wiping her face with her hand. "Samson. I—"

"Would you be less afraid if I left?"

Her eyes widened and her face paled. "Left? Why would you leave?"

He had considered this option. With Tia, he had left her unprotected. He had not wanted to repeat that. But Samson loved Deliliah enough to leave her if that would make her feel safe.

"Would you feel safer?"

Her voice trembled. "No." She spoke more convincingly, almost shouting, "No! You cannot leave!"

She wrapped a corner of her tunic in a knot. "When you left to hunt the lion, I wanted you here. But then I wished you would never return. I don't know what I want. I don't want him to do something to you."

"Who?"

She realized her slip and spoke rapidly as if to distract him. "You wouldn't hurt me. You love me."

"So why won't you trust me to protect you?"

Deliliah's lips trembled. "Because you can't."

"What makes you think I can't?"

Deliliah lowered her eyes. "You're not always here."

Samson tried to understand. "I can take you far from whoever you are afraid of. Would you go with me?"

Deliliah's eyes sparkled, but then died. "I can't leave my father."

"We could take your father and your sister with us." He was as desperate as she to eliminate her fear.

She shook her head. "I could never go far enough. He would find me."

Samson's shoulders slumped. How could he make her trust him? He proceeded with his last option. "If they bind me tightly with new ropes which have never been used, then I will become weak and be like any other man."

Her lips tightened in a straight line and she nodded. Her eyes held a hope he hadn't seen in a long time, yet a dread, too.

He hiked the hillside again. He did not trust his feelings or his actions.

She did not follow.

S amson stretched after dinner. He nodded to Chittem. "Good meal."

Chittem poured hot water into his cup. She covered a yawn. "Can't believe how tired I am."

Abaddon sipped his wine, remaining quiet.

The sun set and shadows darkened the room. The crickets chirped and the cool evening breezes blew in through the windows.

Samson smelled a faint scent of horses. Couldn't they tie them downwind of the house? He shook his head at their foolish attempts at deceit.

Deliliah lit a candle from the cook fire embers.

Abaddon finished his drink. "I must call it a day."

Chittem left too.

Samson yawned and stretched. "Deliliah, I'm tired, too. I think I'll go—"

"No!" She shouted, then tried to calm her voice. "Samson, rest here. I'd feel safer with you here." She smiled.

In spite of her deceit, Samson could not help but be drawn to her smile. He would play his part. He rested his head on her lap as she massaged his head. "You know I let no one touch my head but you."

Deliliah's hands trembled. "I'll be careful not to pull your hair."

Samson closed his eyes and relaxed. He soon breathed deeply, but he did not sleep.

She whispered, her voice like a soft caress. "Samson, can you hear me?"

He did not change his breathing, nor answer her.

He felt the cords tighten around his arms and hands.

He knew what she was doing.

They would be new ropes, never before used. He felt the sudden jerk as she tested the rope a final time.

She raised her voice, "Samson! The Philistines are upon you!"

Samson stood, broke the rope as if it were grass and unsheathed his dagger.

He yanked open the door to the other room and stabbed.

The first man standing behind the door fell. Samson finished all but one before cleaning his knife.

He stepped aside as the last man left. Before he reached the door, Samson spoke, "Only take your horse. The rest are mine."

The man's eyes widened, but he nodded.

Samson watched him go.

A s the moon rose in the night sky, Samson followed the man he had let live. The man was not in any hurry to return to the city to report their failure. Samson grinned in spite of himself. He would find who was behind all of this.

But this time, he felt different. Was he more hesitant and careful? His reflexes were as quick to respond as what he remembered. He remembered his response to his *ima*, "If I didn't instantly react, I'd be dead."

Was there more at stake than before? Is that why he hesitated? It was not. For with the lion, his very life could have been lost.

Had Deliliah's fear squelched his own confidence? Seeing it through someone he loved made the fear real. He did not like how he felt. Is this what his own people felt from the constant raids? No wonder they feared to live!

The rider paused.

Samson reined his own horse.

The city was in sight. And so was the coming sunrise.

He left his horse tied under the trees outside the city in case someone recognized it. He walked the rest of the way.

He stretched his arms over his head and clenched and unclenched his hands. He was ready.

When he entered the city, leaders were gathered in the courtyard. People already stood in line, waiting to have their grievances judged.

Samson paused, looking through the crowd for the horseman. Once he'd spotted him, Samson followed, gliding into doorways and melting into shadows to avoid detection.

There seemed to be more poor and abused people than what he remembered. Or did they stand out more now?

He reached the wider streets where houses were bigger. Their lavish decorations, tall walls, and large barns spoke of wealth. Here the servants were dressed better than most of the common people.

It was at one of these large barns the horseman stopped. He handed his horse to the livery man.

The servant took the horse but shook his head. "He's not here."

The man appeared relieved.

Samson took note of the house. It was the grandest on the street. Samson knew where to come, but not who he should expect. The unknown did not frighten him. He left with greater resolution.

D eliliah rose the next morning with dread. Samson had not spoken nor even looked at her after slaying the Philistines. He had just left. She hurried to the barn to see if he had returned. The straw where he sometimes slept was not disturbed. The barn was empty. She ran to the hilltop to look over the pastures. He had not returned.

She felt loss. What if he did not return? His rejection stung.

She washed before coming to the table. "Have you seen Samson?"

Chittem rolled flatbread. She spit out the words, "Why should he stay? You're a traitor who turned him over to the leaders."

Deliliah sank on the cushions. "Traitor! It's my love for him that tears me to pieces."

"Love? You call that love to ask for his heart's secrets and give them to his enemy?"

Deliliah eyes teared. "Do you know what the leaders will do to me if I don't?"

At Chittem's indifferent shrug, Deliliah wrung her hands. "You don't know what it's like to have a man grab you and take what is most precious from you."

"Bah! Do you think you're the only one they want? Any time I enter the city, I pay my dues at the temple where men wait in line for one who is not wasted like their normal offerings." Chittem shook a flatbread in Deliliah's face. "But you have a man who really loves you. If I had a man like that—" She shook her head.

"What would you do?"

"Trust him to protect me."

"How do I trust?"

"Don't lie to yourself. You do not *want* to trust. You are swayed by the silver in the leaders' hands and so you do not see the love in Samson's eyes."

Deliliah gasped. "How did you know they offered silver?"

"Bah! If they do not hold a dagger to kill you, they bribe with silver. They have no power without something in their hand, because they have nothing in their heart." She paused as she looked toward the door and lowered her voice. "How much did they offer you?"

Deliliah hesitated. Would saying it out loud break its power over her?

"Must've been a lot." Chittem raised her eyebrows.

"They promised 1100 pieces of silver each."

Chittem whistled. "They must believe the stories of Samson's strength! But then, you also saw him defend himself against ten men. What strength! And all because he chose not to leave. Yet you cannot trust him? Yes, you're a traitor."

Deliliah dropped her head. If they could believe his strength, why couldn't she believe he had enough to protect her?

B efore when he had entered a city to do a job such as this, Samson had felt invigorated, empowered by the Spirit of God. Today, he felt different. The Spirit seemed silent. Samson had never asked for His presence. The Spirit merely came in his need. The strength came when he could do no more. He plunged on with his plan. He must do his part and trust for what he could not do.

He reevaluated his actions. The leaders should never control people with fear. It was not just Deliliah's fear, nor just her family's; the herdsman and all their people lived afraid.

Samson paused before their temple. The elaborate steps led to a courtyard where sacrifices were offered. The side rooms housed temple prostitutes. He was not here to offer sacrifices, nor to partake in their offerings. He watched for the one etched in his mind. That man who had come the first time Samson was bound. Samson had let him go as a warning to others. That had been Samson's mistake. Did he control the others?

He leaned in a darkened doorway to watch and wait.

But as the sun rose high in the sky, Samson felt uneasy. He should not be here. Was it just Deliliah's fear influencing him? No, the feeling of unrest was more than that.

He surveyed the streets, kept to the shadows, slunk through the narrow streets, and left the city.

God's strength was not with him.

He didn't know why. It bothered him. He had never asked for it before; it had just come when he needed it.

He should not have come.

He ran back to his horse, mounted, and swung his horse toward home.

Something was wrong.

He must return to Deliliah.

Now.

CHAPTER 21

When Samson reached the hillside, he didn't pause to survey the house or barn. But descending the hill, he saw no movement. He noticed horse droppings outside the doorway. His fears increased. He dismounted and ran into the house.

Chittem turned from the fire with a stick. "He's already gone."

Samson nodded, wishing he had asked Chittem more before. She might have told him answers. "Where's Deliliah?"

Chittem placed a flatbread on the table and motioned for Samson to sit. "Eat."

He didn't feel like eating. He started to leave. Her next words stopped him.

"She's not worthy of your love."

Samson turned back. "Is anyone worthy of love? But God gives it to us."

She laughed. "I don't know of any God's love, but I see yours. I'd go anywhere with that, even if it meant to my death."

Samson paused. Chittem might help him. He sat at the table. "Tell me how to help Deliliah trust me."

"No one can trust for another. And if my sister can't see a man worthy of trust, she is a fool."

"But," Chittem nodded to the flatbread still on the table and placed a bowl beside him. "He who waits for her to trust is more of a fool."

Samson filled the flatbread from the bowl of steaming mutton and gravy. He took a bite. He realized how hungry he was and took another, then chewed. "I am the fool."

Chittem leaned over the table in his face. "Then you will lose."

S amson did not find Deliliah at the barn. Instead he found one ewe lambing. Samson knelt behind the ewe. The lamb's back legs were dangling, but the head seemed stuck. Samson rested his hand on the ewe's back to reassure her. "You know that's not the way to do it, don't you? The head comes first." He pulled as she pushed and released as she stopped. "One more push."

As if she understood, she braced herself for another push. With his help, the lamb came. But the ewe was not finished. Another pair of leg appeared.

"Ahh. You aren't finished. Sorry to disappoint you." Samson resumed his position to help deliver the second lamb.

Deliliah fell to her knees beside him. She wiped the new lamb's nose with the bottom of her tunic. "Creampuff had twins!"

They watched as the ewe licked and nursed both lambs.

Samson faced Deliliah.

Her eyes were red and showed signs of crying. She crossed her arms in a protective position. Her arms were bleeding, as if whipped by a horse's whip.

His anger boiled within him. Before he could speak, she did.

Her voice trembled. "You want me to trust you, but you tell me lies."

Samson wanted to wrap his arms around her and promise to protect her. But he had not been here when she had been whipped. Nor had he kept Tia safe. Who was he to promise safety?

What about the emptiness he had felt in the city? Where was God? His self-doubts escalated.

He had never felt he could *not* do something. He had used all his strength with the lion, but at that moment when he could hold no more, God came.

But this hopelessness would not be resolved by just trying harder or hanging on tighter. He could not change another person. He could not make Deliliah trust. Realizing that was harder to bare than any lion fight.

"Tell me how you can be bound or leave." Deliliah sat in the dirt, waiting his answer.

Samson hung his head at the alternative. If he did leave, she would be hurt, but if he told, he could not protect her. "I will tell you where I get my strength, but only if you trust me to take you away from here."

Deliliah's face paled. She shook her head and ran.

Samson sighed as he watched her go.

CHAPTER 22

The meal was eaten in silence that night. The mutton and gravy Samson had tasted earlier was reheated. The flatbread still good. Abaddon kept his head down and consumed his food without any conversation. Chittem was quiet. Deliliah picked at her food. Samson did not eat much.

Samson nodded. "Chittem, good again."

"Thank you, Samson." Chittem returned the pan to the edge of the coals and left the room.

Deliliah seemed different tonight. Like she had made a decision. She leaned on the cushions. "I don't believe you love me if you won't tell me."

Samson sighed. "You must trust me."

Deliliah shut her eyes as if too heavy to keep open.

Samson sighed, "If you weave my hair with the web and fasten it with a pin, I will become weak like any other man." He looked at her, his eyebrows raised, waiting for her to promise her trust.

She did not.

"Trust goes both ways, Deliliah. You have only what? Silver to gain from my confession? But I have my life to lose by mine. Seems the cost of trust is a bit skewed." Samson rose and kissed her on her head. "I love you." And went to the barn to sleep.

. . .

The next evening, Abaddon and Chittem again left shortly after dinner. Deliliah sat on the cushions as if nothing had happened the evening before. "Come, Samson. Let me brush your hair."

Samson swallowed the feeling of being used. He would not beg for her trust. But he would not run. Could he live with himself if something happened to her because of him? What choice did he have? He lay on her lap.

Samson's heart was no longer in it. He almost felt she deserved what happened to her. Could love be killed by lack of trust? He shook his head.

Deliliah reproved. "Samson, be still. I must start over."

He had forgotten what she was doing. He watched her fingers weave his hair like threads into a cloth.

"Samson, close your eyes. You're making me nervous."

Samson closed his eyes, and finally, he fell sleep.

"Samson! The Philistines are upon you."

He woke and sat. He pulled the pin from his hair and jumped to his feet with his dagger drawn. He opened the door to the next room.

No Philistines waited.

He raised his eyebrows as he looked at Deliliah.

Her expression was of hate.

Samson tossed through the night. He punched the straw as if that would allow him to sleep. It was not about outside fears and what others did anymore. It was about them. What had happened between them? Why wouldn't Deliliah tell him what was wrong? Initially he had just teased her with his wrong answers, to stop her nagging. But her deceit went deeper. Did she wish for his capture? The thought made him stop. What had made her change?

If he killed the leader, it would not repair the trust between them. He knew what he must do. With his decision made, he turned over and slept.

In the morning, Deliliah seemed more distant than ever, as if they had never loved.

They found themselves together with the lambing. One ewe had twins but rejected one. Another ewe had lost her lamb.

Samson skinned the dead lamb and tied its pelt on the rejected lamb so the ewe would smell it as if it were her own and allow it to nurse.

Deliliah pushed the adopted lamb close to the ewe until it nursed.

They worked to save a lamb's life, not considering that their own lives were lost.

When they finished, they sat watching the lambs.

The lambs' antics would have been funny had not Samson's heart felt like breaking. He was so close to Deliliah, yet he had never felt so far from her.

A wall had been built that even he could not destroy.

He closed his eyes. What a paradox life was.

Deliliah broke into his thoughts; her voice flat and lifeless. "How can you say, 'I love you,' when your heart is not with me? You have deceived me these three times and have not told me where your strength is."

Samson did not recognize his own voice, "A razor has never touched my head, for I have been a Nazirite to God from my mother's womb. If I am shaved, my strength will be gone."

He stood, without speaking anything more, and hiked the hillside to watch the sunset alone.

A fter Samson confessed, Deliliah watched him leave. At another time, she would have longed never to leave his side and would have watched the sunset with him. But tonight, all she felt was empty.

He had finally told her the truth. She knew it.

After all that begging, she thought it would be something great. Perhaps to the Jews, it was. But cutting his hair!

Getting the answer was not what she expected. She had thought she would feel relief. Or happiness. She could go anywhere with that much money. And be safe.

But she felt nothing.

She returned to the house.

Chittem stood over the fire. "Are you two ready to eat? I've kept the food warm."

Deliliah glanced at the food and wrinkled her nose. "I'm not hungry."

"Will Samson eat? Should I wait?"

Deliliah shrugged, looking at the door. "I doubt it. Go to bed, Chittem."

"What happened between you two? You both look like you died."

Deliliah sighed. "Maybe you're right."

D eliliah had convinced the messenger this was the real secret. Being confident of its success, she had even demanded payment before the evening. She would soon be free and escape Hadid's clutches and go anywhere.

Yet a nagging fear lingered. Would she really be free?

Deliliah ignored the doubt and counted her silver. The coins sifted through her fingers to the pile on her bed. Even with the silver in her possession, she felt no freedom from the fear that gripped her heart.

She rose to meet Samson in the main room.

It would soon be over.

He sat beside her.

His touch felt mechanical, without the magic that held her before.

He lay in her lap.

Deliliah's hands trembled as she brushed Samson's hair with her fingers.

This would be the last time.

He had trusted her with his secret.

Samson opened his eyes and smiled. It seemed forced. Like he was offering a sacrifice of his own choosing.

She shut her eyes to avoid looking into his soul.

But she couldn't shut her ears to his words. "I fought my cousin when I was twelve just because he touched my hair." He shook his head.

Her fingers got tangled in his locks when he did.

She swallowed the lump in her throat but couldn't answer.

He continued, "Look how far I've fallen! To tell a Philistine the secret to my strength!" He closed his eyes. His expression showed peace.

His breathing deepened.

Deliliah brought out the shears hidden under her cushion. But she could not bring herself to cut his hair. "Hadid!"

He opened the door where the others waited. He appeared distrustful and displeased.

Deliliah handed him the shears. "You must cut his hair. I can't."

Hadid grabbed the shears, pulled Samson's locks and snipped them short.

Deliliah watched them drop to the floor. The long locks that had identified Samson his entire life were gone in a snip. Lifeless. Dead. She gulped.

Hadid shaved Samson's head.

Deliliah shook herself out of her concentration when she saw his head. "You didn't have to make him bald, just shorten his hair!"

Hadid hissed. "I'll take no chances. Now wait until I'm behind that door, before you wake him."

The door closed quietly.

Deliliah swallowed. What had she done?

Why hadn't he woken already? She watched his chest rise and fall in slumber, his face at peace.

She bent to kiss his lips. "Forgive me, Samson. I have taken your heart and I wasn't worthy of it. You would have found a way to protect me."

But he did not hear.

She shouted, "The Philistines are upon you, Samson!"

He woke and stood.

When the men came from the room, he had barely drawn his dagger.

Deliliah watched in horror as the men surrounded him and beat him. What had she done? She wanted to shout, "Protect yourself!" But she could only watch as if in some warped dream.

When the men continued beating him even after he had fallen to the ground, Deliliah screamed, "Stop!"

But they did not listen.

His body lay in a crumbled heap. Blood pooled under him.

"Hold him steady." Hadid took his dagger. His face reflected a demonic glee. "He will never wreck my plans nor my people again." He looked at Deliliah.

Deliliah covered her face but could not mute Samson's screams as Hadid gouged out his eyes.

"Tie him behind my horse," Hadid commanded.

Deliliah watched them leave. She stood long after she could no longer see their dust on the road.

Chittem stood beside her. "I hope you're happy."

Deliliah put her head down. "Why shouldn't I be?"

"Because you killed the only man who ever loved you."

"I *did not* cut his hair."

Chittem shook her head. "Do not deceive yourself. You might as well have stabbed him in the heart."

Deliliah said nothing, but in bed that night she cried for what could never be again.

CHAPTER 23

S amson did not remember much of the trip to the city. Though his captors debated about taking him to Sorek or Gaza, he did not care. Both towns knew him for his destruction.

He was bound and thrown in a dungeon.

He did not know how long he lay on the cold, damp, dirt floor before he realized he was no longer being dragged behind the horse. Moving was agony. Chains dug into his ankles, rubbing them raw. He passed into a tormented sleep. His wounds throbbed, then festered. Several ribs were broken. Breathing was an effort. Coughing painful. When he spit, after coughing, his mouth tasted of blood. He licked his lips. They burned.

But lying there was better than when came after. He was barely able to stand when they unchained him from the post and dragged him to the grind stone. There he was chained again to a beam meant for an ox, and forced to walk in circles, working the heavy grindstones. He could smell the freshly ground wheat, but he could not eat of it. To faltered or slow brought a whip to his back. A bone poked through his foot. Walking brought excruciating pain.

As Samson walked in circles, he laughed at the irony of grinding wheat the Philistine had stolen from his own people. A humorless laugh.

He had wanted to live life. Isn't that what had frustrated him about his own people?

When had he stopped pursing life?

When had he lost the Lord's strength?

Was it when he shared God's secret with a foreigner? Or had it left long before that?

He remembered sunsets, vibrant across the sky, rich colors changing to dark hues as the sun disappeared.

He thought of the fires from the foxes spreading across wheat fields.

He thought of the men whose wardrobes had fulfilled his wager.

He thought of the elderly couple who had met his need.

He thought of his father. His *abba* had understood him. He was one of the few who believed him to be the deliverer of his people.

What had he told him? "You are not alone."

He grunted. If he had stayed alone, he might be better off.

His heart was gone. His strength was gone. And his life was not worth much.

If he could have cried, he would have.

By loving a woman who didn't respect him, he found something worse than living—a living death.

S amson had just been returned to his cell.

The guard threw in his food. The mush glumped and splattered on the floor.

Samson listened to where it landed, so he could find it before something else ate it. The gruel resembled sawdust, but Samson ate it, licking what he could off the ground. The vessel pushed inside his door was neither wine nor tea, but water—it smelled of the streets. He took one gulp and licked his lips. Though thirsty, he must keep some for later when his sore throat was unbearable. He leaned against the stone wall, settling down for the night, though he knew sleep would not be soon in coming.

It was in these long moments prior to sleep that his mind troubled him. He thought over his life and what he had done.

The strength of killing the lion and moving a gate seemed so far away now. Had God really used him to do those things?

Why couldn't he call this strength when he wanted it?

Wasn't that what his people expected—to be shown God's strength at their whim?

But God wasn't for show.

Samson licked his lips again and rested his head against the wall. How he wished for water! A drip seeped between the stones and wet his head. He stretched around and licked it. It tasted better than the streets' offerings.

He no longer spoke. It was like being in a silent tomb.

His ears worked, unlike his eyes, but there was nothing to hear, except the animals that stole his food.

He scratched his head—the only place on his body that did not ache. It itched. His hair was growing back.

He smiled, ironic.

His prison door squeaked open. The draft brought moans from others who shared similar fates.

The jailor unlocked the chains that bound his feet, pushed him to his feet, and dragged him toward the door.

"Where are you taking me?" His voice was scratchy and distorted. He did not recognize his own voice.

The jailor would not say.

Samson stumbled as the jailor dragged him. He fell against the wall to get his balance. Each step brought pain.

The jailor yanked up his arm chains when they reached stairs. "Hurry."

They reached another door, where he was pushed through it.

Samson smelled air that was not putrid or rancid. He filled his lungs with it, in spite of the pain breathing brought.

The jailor must not be taking him to grind wheat. He was handed over to others. Their clanking armor told Samson they were soldiers.

Another door squeaked open.

He was pushed out.

A cheer arose. A chant. "Our god has given our enemy into our hands, even the destroyer of our country, who has slain many of us."

The song stopped as Samson was pushed into their midst.

He was in the street, surrounded now by the babble of voices.

So used the quietness of his own thoughts, the noise was almost too much.

Yanked by his chains to his feet, he was prodded like an animal to keep walking.

People crowded on either side of him, pushing, spiting, taunting, and teasing.

Though he could not retaliate nor see his abusers, he smiled at their taunts. They seemed petty compared to the destruction he had brought by the Hand of God upon them.

His smile made them abuse him more.

He stumbled and fell.

They kicked him. Someone stepped on his chains, preventing him from standing.

The crowd fell on him, pelting him from all directions.

He tried to duck his head beneath his arms to protect it.

Finally, soldiers cleared the mob and dragged him to a place apart.

He was alone. He leaned against a pillar breathing deeply. He licked his lips; bleeding. Wounds had opened.

The voices could be heard above him.

Samson felt a foreboding. The hair rose on his neck.

He heard a breathe beside him. "Who stands by me?"

The voice was a boy's. "I alone. To keep you here."

Samson grunted—a mere lad to watch the one who was once the strongest man in their midst. He asked, but did not need an answer, "Where am I?"

"The temple."

His shoulders slumped. His humiliation would be complete.

Someone shouted over the balcony, "Move Samson where we can see him."

He was pulled by his chains. He knew what to expect. He remembered. He stood in a courtyard below the balcony for people to watch.

The pressure on his chains released.

He stood alone.

Though he could not see, he felt exposed and naked. His blood seeping from his wounds, tickled his skin, making him itch.

He threw his shoulders back, in spite of the pain it brought to breathe. He would stand proud, though his insides quivered at what awaited him.

Something hit him. He yielded to the impact. It dripped down his body to fall by his feet. He smelled decaying onions and waste. If he had eaten any substantial food, he would have lost it. Another mass hit him in the mouth and stung his lips. Before he could think, he licked them. Rotten figs. He wanted to spit it out, but would not give them the satisfaction.

Figs reminded him of his *ima's* fig spread. He concentrated on that and smiled.

His smile incited the crowd's fury. But they soon grew weary of him when they could not make him respond.

His chains grew taut.

"Come this way," the lad commanded.

He sloshed through refuse. Though he could not see, in his mind's eye, he relived the night when he first saw the Philistine's temple: the naked man chained and led by a child, exposed, humiliated, abused, tormented.

It hadn't taken much to switch places.

No wonder God had told His people to destroy them! There was nothing worth saving. Except maybe Tia and Deliliah. But they too would not see God.

When he reached a pillar, he leaned against it. He sensed the boy standing within hearing distance. "Show me another pillar, so I may stand."

Rather than touch his body, the boy dragged his chain until his hand bumped the pillar.

Samson struggled to stand, leaning on both pillars for support. The effort left him breathing deeply.

What would become of the deliverer of God's people? Was this it? A life of mindless grinding wheat and groveling in the dirt for food? Or would he end up on the altar to their god?

He grunted. To begin life blessed of God. To end life sacrificed to man's pleasure. He could not endure that. Samson cried, "O Lord God, please remember me and give me strength just one more time, that I may be avenged of these Philistines for my two eyes."

He pushed on the two middle pillars, much like when he had taken the city gate to the top of the hill. But this time, he felt no exhilarating power, only intense pain. When he felt the pillars shift, he added to his prayer, "Let me die with the Philistines."

The pillars moved.

Samson heard screams. He felt the impact as he was crushed by the balcony. And he knew no more.

Samson died, surrounded by three thousand people, alone, but not forsaken by God.

EPILOGUE

After Samson was captured, Deliliah could only hear again and again Samson's screams as his eyes were taken from him. She could not bear to enter the room where they still lay on the floor. She flung the silver from her bed. The coins rolled all over her room, clattering loudly before spiraling into silence. Why had they seemed like the answer?

Perhaps Chittem was right; perhaps love could have won.

But she would never know that now.

Hadid returned for her.

Her mind told her to flee—but her body felt hollow and empty, as if something good had drained from it. She was not afraid, only resigned. Maybe this was her payment.

She approached Hadid without hesitation.

His eyes widened perhaps surprised by her willingness.

She would live wishing for the death she had given to Samson.

Z'llpunith pushed away the bowl of ground wheat and looked up as her grandchildren ran toward her. "Guess what we heard?"

Z'llpunith laughed. "What?"

The two children argued, "Don't tell her. Let me."

Finally, the youngest blurted out, "Samson is dead."

Z'llpunith's hands trembled

Tad followed behind them.

She looked at him. "Is it true?"

Tad expression softened. "We heard at the village."

Z'llpunith's voice grew soft. "Then I guess it's over."

Tad hugged her. "Samson's death caused quite a stir among the Philistines. They say over 3,000 lords and leaders from all the cities around Gaza had gathered to celebrate Samson's capture. He pushed down the temple's pillars and crashed the entire building. They say, by his death, he killed more than those he killed in his life."

Z'llpunith swallowed. "He has done what he came to do." She looked at Tad. "You must go for his body."

"Me? He's in the Philistine's lands!"

Z'llpunith nodded. "Manoah would want Samson to be buried with him."

Tad swallowed. "I will go."

When Samson's body was brought back to the village, no one attended the burial except Tad and Z'llpunith. She squeezed Tad's hand after he threw the last dirt on the grave. "Thank you. You've done what you were supposed to do."

Tad nodded and left.

Z'llpunith stayed at the grave site. She would be the only one to mourn his passing.

Not one of his own would accept him for who he was, not even in his death.

Samson was the son who removed the barren curse from his mother, but he in turn became the curse of his people.

His appearance did not indicate any strength.

He was despised and rejected by his own.

He was betrayed by those he loved.

Samson delivered his people for twenty years, but his people did not acknowledge him.

He died alone, but even in his death he was not forsaken by God.

His life, though stained with sin, foretold of Someone Who would come later to truly deliver His people from their bondage.

GLOSSARY

Abba – Hebrew, endearing form of father

Cubit – form of ancient measurement, length from middle finger tip to elbow bottom; about 18 inches

Ima – Hebrew for mother

Jennet – donkey, female

Lafa – Hebrew for flatbread

Matza – Jewish, unleavened flatbread

Sava – Hebrew for grandmother

Shalom – Jewish greeting at meeting or parting; means "peace"

Shearling – year-old sheep that has been shorn once

SUMMARY REMARKS

Judges didn't judge. In most cases they became the military leader, bringing a group into battle against those who oppressed them. In the case of Samson, he didn't solicit others to follow him; he fought on his own. In fact, his own people were willing to turn him over to their enemies. In the case of Deborah, she wasn't the battle leader, but she did remind the people of what the Law said.

Israel at this time was not a united political entity with a strong leader. They operated as tribes or groups of tribes, similar to the "confederation of states" in American history. Each judge affected only a region of Israel.

The book of Judges fills the gap of Israel's history between Joshua and Samuel. It also sets the stage for the book of Ruth. In those days, everyone did that which was right in their own eyes. Because of this setting, Ruth's retelling of the Kinsman-Redeemer has more significance. While everyone cared not for God or anyone else, the redeemer saved Ruth. The contrast brings grace and salvation to life.

God destroyed evil; He did not negotiate with it. He ordered complete annihilation of the people who lived in Israel before His people settled. The Canaanites were wicked, ripe for His judgment. By their presence, they caused God's people to sin.

It wasn't being a foreigner that merited annihilation. God

welcomed those who embraced Israel's faith, such as Tamar, Rahab and Ruth, all foreigners who became part of the Messianic line.

God also allowed the Philistines, Canaanites, Sidonians and Hivites to remain in the land to test Israel and teach them war (Judges 3:1-4).

Government's duty is to execute judgment upon evildoers. Instead, the inhabitants of the land rewarded injustices and favored cruelty.

Israel had no formal government to execute justice, but instead followed in the sins of those inhabitants that remained in the land.

Just as God didn't permit sin in those who inhabited the land before His people, so God didn't allow it in His own people. Judges shows this cycle with God's own people. They sinned, God punished them by allowing the heathens to oppress them, and they turned to God for salvation from their suffering.

Many have tried to construct a timeline to help explain the disjointedness of the judges. No chronology adequately explains the time required for people's fall into sin, their suffering, and their salvation as does Dr. Gerald Aardsma with his chronology explanation.

I refer you to his research at BiblicalChronologist.org. But by brief explanation, if a thousand years is added to the book of Judges, the date of the Exodus becomes 2450 BC, substantiating archeological finds and radiocarbon dating without doing extensive gymnastics with the Biblical text as some scholars have tried to do to make the facts correspond to the Biblical account.

Another question is how Samuel fits into the timeline. Does he follow all the judges or reign simultaneously with the latter judges?

Although I wish to be as accurate as possible in what I present, both archeologically and biblically, I do take fictitious liberties to write a story.

In the Biblical account, Samson's mother's name is not given.

In Leviticus 15:19-33, a woman was required to offer two turtle-doves or two young pigeons to the priest after a discharge. One bird was offered for a sin offering; the other for a burnt offering. It was unclear to me whether it referred to all women with a discharge of blood, or only the woman who discharged outside the period of her menstruation.

Deuteronomy 7:3-4 says, "Furthermore, you shall not intermarry with them [those in the land]; you shall not give your daughters to their sons, nor shall you take their daughters for your sons. For they will turn your sons away from following Me to serve other gods; then the anger of the Lord will be kindled against you and He will quickly destroy you."

In Chapter 13, the Psalm of Moses was Psalm 90:4, "For a thousand years in Your sight are like yesterday when it passes by."

FEELING ALONE?

You've tried to be strong. But you can't.

You've tried to be good. But you aren't.

The Bible already told us we couldn't. It says, *"For all have sinned and fall short of the glory of God"* (Romans 3:23).

Trying harder only brings bondage, and suffering. for *"the wages of sin is death"* (Romans 6:23).

We have ignored God.

God has not forgotten you. He's waiting for you to acknowledge your need of Him. He provided a way for us to be strong and good, but only through His Son, Who paid the penalty for our sin and became sin for us, so we could be like Him, sinless and strong through His Spirit. *"But God demonstrates His own love toward us, in that while we were yet sinners, Christ died for us"* (Romans 5:8).

God brings us out of bondage when we repent, acknowledging Him. *"Call to Me and I will answer you"* (Jeremiah 33:3).

"Cleanse me from my sin. For I know my transgressions, and my sin is ever before me. Against You (God), You only, I have sinned. . . Wash me and I shall be whiter than snow. . . Create in me a clean heart, O God, and renew a steadfast spirit within me. Do not cast me away from Your presence and do not take Your Holy Spirit from me" (Psalm 51).

When we look to God, we find hope.

When we turn to Him, we are freed from our bondage.

When we remember Him, we are changed, by His Spirit working in us, to imitate His Son.

Don't keep trying to do it on your own and ignore Him.

Call on Him today.

THANK YOU

If you have enjoyed *Alone But not Forsaken,* help spread the word. Post a review (how you liked it and why).

What is a reviewer?

Someone who reads my book and tells others what they thought of it.

What do you do?

1.Read the book.

2.Write three sentences about the book.

a. The What sentence: summarizes the book.

b. The Why sentence: tells what the book did for you, why others should read it, why you chose to read it. Example: you wanted to see God's strength.

c. The How sentence: tells how well you liked the book.

3.Post your review here:

www.goodreads.com

www.sonyacontreras.com

And places where you have purchased it.

Please allow me to use your review for marketing. Include a note in your message giving me permission.

BIBLIOGRAPHY

Bible Hub. (2018, June 12). *Zorah*. Retrieved June 2018, from Bible Atlas: http://bibleatlas.org/full/zorah.htm

Broyles, S. (2005, November). *The Dog: Its Gradually Changing Status*. Retrieved June 2018, from The Andreas Center: http://www.andreascenter.org/Articles/Dog.htm

Deffinbaugh, B. (2004, May 18). *The Clean and Unclean Part 1 (Leviticus 11)*. Retrieved June 2018, from Bible. Org: https://bible.org/seriespage/8-clean-and-unclean-part-i-leviticus-11

Hebrew Baby Names. (n.d.). Retrieved 2018, from Baby Name Guide: http://www.babynameguide.com/categoryhebrew.asp?   strGender=M&strAlpha=B&strCat=Hebrew&strOrder=Name

Honeybees:Jewish Connection. (n.d.). Retrieved June 2018, from Chabad.org: https://www.chabad.org/kids/noahsark/animal_c-do/aid/533900/jewish/Honeybees.htm

Hyndman, R. (2011, November 20). *Who Were the Gileadites*. Retrieved March 2018, from Bible Questions Answered: http://bibleq.net/answer/4851/

Isachar, H. (n.d.). *Trees of the Holy Land*. Retrieved June 2018, from Hanan Isachar Photography: https://isachar-photography.photoshelter.com/gallery-collection/Trees-of-the-Holy-Land/C00004SLXR6DKC28

Lehnardt, K. (2016, December 28). *Roaring Lion Facts*. Retrieved June 2018, from Fact Retriever: https://www.factretriever.com/lions

Lemos, T. M. (n.d.). *Weddings and Marriage Traditions in Ancient Israel.* Retrieved June 2018, from Bible Odyssey: http://www.bibleodyssey. org/passages/related-articles/weddings-and-marriage-traditions-in-ancient-israel

Lewis, A. H. (1996, October 31). The Strong Character of Samson's Mother. *Priscilla Papers: The Academic Journal of CBE International, 10*(4), pp.   https://www.cbeinternational.org/resources/article/priscilla-papers/strong-character-samson's-mother.

Lions of Africa: Hunting. (n.d.). Retrieved June 2018, from Chakarov: http://www.chakarov.com/studentswork/lions/hunting.html

Matthew Henry Commentary. (n.d.). *Judges 11.* Retrieved March 2018, from Bible Study Tools: https://www.biblestudytools.com/ commentaries/matthew-henry- complete/judges/11.html

Neumer, S. (2015, August 24). *Israel's Ten Most Beautiful Animals.* Retrieved June 2018, from From the Grapevine: https://www. fromthegrapevine.com/nature/israels-10-beautiful- animals

Norris, A. (2014, August 12). *Ten Incredible Desert Animals That Can Take the Heat.* Retrieved June 2018, from From the Grapevine: https:// www.fromthegrapevine.com/slideshows/nature/10-desert-animals-israel

Predator Behaviour. (n.d.). Retrieved June 2018, from Lion Alert: http://lionalert.org/page/predatory-behaviour

Rotem. (2018, April 28). *Usha.* Retrieved September 2018, from Bible Walks: https://biblewalks.com/Sites/Usha.html#East

Rotem. (2019, June 6). *Trees and Bushes.* Retrieved 2019, from Bible Walks: https://biblewalks.com/Info/Trees.html

Rudd, S. (n.d.). *The Three Stage Ritual of Bible Marriages.* Retrieved June 2018, from Bible CA: http://www.bible.ca/marriage/ancient-jewish-three-stage-weddings-and-marriage-customs-ceremony-in-the-bible.htm

Tsimbler, L. (n.d.). *Herbs and Spices in Israel.* Retrieved December 2017, from Israel: https://www.israel-in-photos.com/herbs-and-spices.html

What Is the Meaning of Shibboleth in the Bible? (n.d.). Retrieved March 2018, from Got Questions?: https://www.biblestudytools.com/ commentaries/matthew-henry- complete/judges/12.html

ABOUT THE AUTHOR

Sonya Contreras grew up living with five sisters. Her mom was like a worker bee who did not quit. She learned not only to rise early to have the bathroom, but that the emotional tension of tight quarters *could* bring harmony out of chaos—by nothing short of the work of God. Her parents provided stability that showed her a God Who was immutable.

Her high school science teacher taught her to ask God even when she didn't like the answer. He showed her a God Who was faithful.

Studying at Cedarville University and Institute for Creation Research Graduate Program grounded her roots in God's truth from His Word *and* His world. She found that God's power and wisdom created and sustained.

Teaching high school science opened her eyes to see the suffering of her world, but also saw a God Who suffered with them.

She was thrown into a world of men by her husband and God when they were given eight sons. Only by God's power and patience do she and her husband direct their sons' wanderings in truth and love. Small steps, big hearts, treasured memories. Their eight boys learn to be men with convictions, courage, and skills.

God held her hand as she learned of His steadfastness and faithfulness. But raising her boys has caused her to grab hold of His Hand and not let go. She has found a God Who wanted her to know Him.

How does she tell about herself? She tells of her God Who is forgiving, faithful, and desires her friendship. She writes of Him and for Him; for without Him, she could do nothing and be nothing.

Read more at sonyacontreras.com

ALSO BY SONYA CONTRERAS

Tell of My Kingdom's Glory Series tells the love story between God and His people.

In **Book One:** *Until My Name Is Known,* God brings His people to see Him as He frees them from the bonds of Egypt. Read it to see God.

In **Book Two:** *I Have Called You by Name,* God draws His people to know Him, as He provides safety through the demands of His Law and teaches dependence upon Him to reach their Land. Read it to know God.

In **Book Three:** *I Am with You,* God reassures His people that, as He had been with Moses, so would He be with them. He brings them into the Land promised them, giving rest from their journey. Read it to rest in God.

He Has Not Forgotten Series Though God's people have forgotten Him, He has not forgotten them. He raises up judges for their deliverance.

In **Book One:** *But You Have Not Obeyed Me,* God's people forget God. Short stories of the first judges show how much they've forgotten. But when they cry to Him, God sends them deliverers. Read these stories to see why man needs God.

In **Book Two:** *Alone, But Not Forsaken,* God will not be ignored. He prepares Samson to deliver His people from their bondage. Watch God use one man to show the world His strength.

Expecting Jesus

See Jesus through the eyes of those who met Him.

Our Story of His Lessons: Twenty Years of Christmas News

People ask about our boys and how we do it. The yearly letters found here give you a glimpse into those answers.

Let Her Hear: Parables from a Mom

Devotionals to give that glimpse of the heavenly realm through the struggles of earthly life.

Faith Like a Mustard Seed

Cultivate that mustard seed faith by knowing the Saviour and watch your mountains move.

How Suffering Shows God's Love: A Paradox Explained

Pain searches for meaning. Questions bring us to God. We discover the God Who wants us to know Him.

For a complete and current listing of books with excerpts see www.sonyacontreras.com

Sign up to receive weekly articles.

I write about what matters to you—women, wives, and moms—about your family, faith and future. I write about what's hard, what helps, what heals. I show you how it's done. And not done. I hold your hand as you find what matters to the Savior. And let go of those things that mattered to you, but not to Him. I write about what matters to Him.